She waited, giving him a chance to confess

She wanted him to offer a good excuse for why he'd screwed up his carburetor, why he'd pretended to need a mechanic, why he'd been looking for Charlie Larkin in the first place.

She could see the battle going on in his eyes. Deep dark blue eyes like the bottom of the ocean. She watched him clench his hands into fists, his broad, muscular back to her, suddenly making her take notice of his size. Her gaze dropped to the jeans he wore and the muscled legs she could make out through the denim. A flicker of heat a lot like desire found flame inside her. He walked away from her so swiftly that she was startled.

But she knew that wasn't what she had to fear from Gus Riley. It was the way he made her feel. Vulnerable, the way an animal can sense weakness in his prey. It was as if Gus could see beneath the baggy clothing to that unfulfilled ache deep within her like an Achilles' heel.

And that couldn't have been more dangerous to her....

Dear Harlequin Intrigue Reader,

We've got what you need to start the holiday season with a *bang*. Starting things off is RITA® Award-winning author Gayle Wilson. Gayle returns to Harlequin Intrigue with a spin-off of her hugely popular MEN OF MYSTERY series. Same sexy heroes, same drama and danger...but with a new name! Look for *Rafe Sinclair's Revenge* under the PHOENIX BROTHERHOOD banner.

You can return to the royal kingdom of Vashmira in *Royal Ransom* by Susan Kearney, which is the second book in her trilogy THE CROWN AFFAIR. This time an American goes undercover to protect the princess. But will his heart be exposed in the process?

B.J. Daniels takes you to Montana to encounter one very tough lady who's about to meet her match in a mate. Only thing...can he avoid the deadly fate of her previous beaux? Find out in *Premeditated Marriage*.

Winding up the complete package, we have a dramatic story about a widow and her child who become targets of a killer, and only the top cop can keep them out of harm's way. Linda O. Johnston pens an emotionally charged story of crime and compassion in *Tommy's Mom*.

Make sure you pick up all four, and please let us know what you think of our brand of breathtaking romantic suspense.

Enjoy!

Sincerely,

Denise O'Sullivan
Associate Senior Editor
Harlequin Intrigue

PREMEDITATED MARRIAGE

B.J. DANIELS

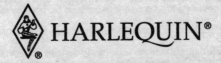

TORONTO • NEW YORK • LONDON
AMSTERDAM • PARIS • SYDNEY • HAMBURG
STOCKHOLM • ATHENS • TOKYO • MILAN • MADRID
PRAGUE • WARSAW • BUDAPEST • AUCKLAND

ISBN 0-373-22687-X

PREMEDITATED MARRIAGE

Copyright © 2002 by Barbara Heinlein

All rights reserved. Except for use in any review, the reproduction or utilization of this work in whole or in part in any form by any electronic, mechanical or other means, now known or hereafter invented, including xerography, photocopying and recording, or in any information storage or retrieval system, is forbidden without the written permission of the publisher, Harlequin Enterprises Limited, 225 Duncan Mill Road, Don Mills, Ontario, Canada M3B 3K9.

All characters in this book have no existence outside the imagination of the author and have no relation whatsoever to anyone bearing the same name or names. They are not even distantly inspired by any individual known or unknown to the author, and all incidents are pure invention.

This edition published by arrangement with Harlequin Books S.A.

® and TM are trademarks of the publisher. Trademarks indicated with ® are registered in the United States Patent and Trademark Office, the Canadian Trade Marks Office and in other countries.

Visit us at www.eHarlequin.com

Printed in U.S.A.

ABOUT THE AUTHOR

B.J. Daniels sets her latest book in the backwoods of Montana, a place she knows well. She's lived in Montana since she was five, when her family moved to a cabin her father built in the Gallatin Canyon.

A former award-winning journalist, B.J. had thirty-six short stories published before she wrote and sold her first romantic suspense, *Odd Man Out,* which was later nominated for the *Romantic Times* Reviewer's Choice Award for Best First Book and Best Harlequin Intrigue.

B.J. lives in Bozeman with her husband, Parker, two springer spaniels, Zoey and Scout, and an irascible tomcat named Jeff. She is a member of the Bozeman Writers Group and Romance Writers of America. To contact her, write P.O. Box 183, Bozeman, MT 59771.

Books by B.J. Daniels

HARLEQUIN INTRIGUE

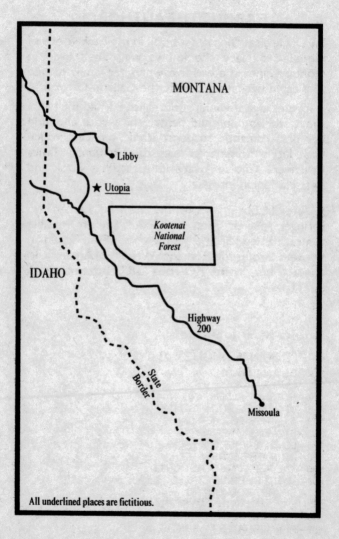

MONTANA

● Libby

★ <u>Utopia</u>

*Kootenai
National
Forest*

IDAHO

Highway
200

*State
Border*

● Missoula

All underlined places are fictitious.

CAST OF CHARACTERS

Augustus T. Riley—The true-crime writer specializes in women who kill their lovers, and now he has Charlotte "Charlie" Larkin in his sights.

Charlotte "Charlie" Larkin—She thought her luck with men was bad. But Augustus T. Riley proves it can get a whole lot worse....

Trudi Murphy—She has a lot to offer men—and does.

Quinn Simonson—He and "Charlie" were high school sweethearts until his car missed a turn on the lake road.

Phil Simonson—The chain-saw artist blames Charlotte for his son's death.

Jenny Lee-Simonson—Jenny Lee was Charlotte's best friend until she married into the Simonson family.

Forest Simonson—Is his hatred of Charlotte only because of his brother's death? Or is there more to it?

Josh Whitacker—Everyone wants to know how his body ended up at the bottom of the lake.

Wayne Dreyer—He's devoted to more than the old Chevy his father gave him.

T. J. Blue—Is he just the strong, silent type? Or is he hiding something?

Vera Larkin—Charlotte's mother is sicker than she knows, and her daughter is determined to protect her.

Selma Royal—Everyone believes the old maid can see the future. But what does she see for her niece Charlie?

Rickie Moss—He learned the hard way what getting close to Charlotte "Charlie" Larkin could cost him.

Earlene Kurtz—Everyone in town knew she was pregnant with Quinn Simonson's baby seven years ago, including Charlotte.

This book is dedicated to my Aunt Susie
in Houston, Texas, in memory of the love of her life,
her hero and husband, T. O. Gressett.

Prologue

The warm harvest moon cast a silver sheen over the lake and the naked young lovers standing waist deep in the still summer-warm water. Just yards away, crouched in the darkness of the pines, a lone figure watched, trying to decide whether to kill them both now—or wait.

They shouldn't have been here.

No one came up the weed-choked road to Freeze Out Lake anymore. Not after all the tragedies. No one was fool enough to come near the place late at night—let alone swim in the eerie dark waters.

Except for these two.

They began to stroke each other, their mouths hungry as their hands caressed wet bodies shimmering in the moonlight, the boy's shoulders muscled, the girl's breasts large and white, bobbing in the water.

The boy lured her out deeper into the lake in a sort of sex-driven tag where he dived beneath the water, making the girl giggle and pretend to fight him off, daring her to swim farther and farther from the shore.

The lake was low, lower than it had been in years because of the recent drought, making it dangerously shallow.

The boy swam away from her, calling for her to follow him as he dived and splashed. But a few dozen yards from the shore, the boy disappeared under the water and the girl slowed as if sensing the danger.

Suddenly the boy surfaced like a porpoise. "Hey!" he called, his voice a little unsteady. "There's something out here!"

"What is it?" The girl stopped swimming.

Letting them live was no longer an option.

"What is it?" the girl called again, alarm in her voice.

"I don't know." He sounded scared now, his voice rising, echoing off the bank of trees that surrounded the small, remote lake. "Whatever it is, I'm standing on part of it." Sealing his fate, he disappeared beneath the surface.

The girl continued to tread water, her attention on the spot where the boy had vanished, seemingly unaware of the movement in the trees behind her. A branch cracked in the underbrush.

She jerked her head around, her gaze riveting on a spot in the trees, a look of alarm skewing her expression as if she'd seen something moving through the darkness toward her and the boy.

The rumble of a vehicle off in the distance distracted her for just an instant—just long enough that when she focused again on the spot in the trees, it was clear she no longer saw movement. But it was also clear from the look on her face that she saw *something*. Maybe the shape of the person standing in the shadows of the pines at the edge of the moon-drenched shore. Or maybe just the glint of the filet knife's long, sharp blade.

Abruptly the boy's head broke the surface in a spray of silver droplets. He began to swim in wild, frantic strokes toward the shore and the pile of clothing so carelessly discarded earlier.

"What's wrong?" the girl cried. "What is it?"

"Get out of the water!" the boy screamed, his moonlit face twisted in horror as he beat the water with his arms and legs, swimming madly for the shore and what he foolishly thought would be safety.

The sound of an engine grew louder. Someone was coming up the lake road. Lights flickered erratically through the dark branches just before a pickup burst out into the open, stopping at the edge of the water.

"Oh God, it's my dad!" the girl gulped. She was still yards from shore and her clothing—trapped and naked as sin.

The unforgiving moon illuminated her as she sunk, neck deep in the water, neck deep in trouble. But she would never know just how much trouble she'd really been in—before her father had showed up.

He slammed out of his pickup, a shotgun in his beefy hands and guttural curses spewing from his wide mouth like bullets.

But the boy didn't seem to notice the gun or his own nakedness as he lurched from the water, choking out something about a car in the middle of the lake—and a body.

In the dark shadows of the pines, the knife blade glittered for only an instant before disappearing back into its sheath. By morning the sheriff's department would have dragged the car from the lake and found what was left of the body strapped behind the wheel. Nothing to be done about that now.

Chapter One

October 8

The headlights drilled a hole through the dark, exposing what finally looked like a place to pull over.

Augustus T. Riley braked and swung the rental car into the narrow patch of dirt on the right side of the highway. He hadn't seen a car in hours—just miles of nothing but old two-lane blacktop banked by towering pines now etched ebony against the moonless sky.

Once stopped, he sat for a moment, the dark night closing in around him, the headlights doing little to ward it off. He'd never known such darkness, certainly not where he was from. And certainly not this early—just a little after seven. Over the murmur of the car engine, he heard the *whoop whoop* of wings an instant before something flew through the pale path of the headlamps and disappeared into the woods.

Damn, this country was desolate.

Turning on the dome light, he checked the map. He couldn't be more than a few miles from the town.

The drive had been long and gruelling, and not surprisingly, he was hungry and tired.

Once he got there, he'd have little to go on. Little more than a name and a phone number. But he'd gotten by with far less in the past.

Refolding the map, he shoved it into his briefcase out of sight and, leaving the engine running, climbed out. The night air was colder than he'd anticipated and cut through his lightweight jacket, sending a chill skittering across his skin. He caught the rank smell of something dead and decomposing. Roadkill. Fortunately, he couldn't see what was lying in the tall weeds where the putrid odor emanated. Didn't want to. Probably a wild animal. A coyote. Or a deer.

Whatever it was, it had been dead for some time.

He shivered as he went to the front of the car, popped the hood and leaned in.

From the darkness came a hushed moan that made him jerk up in surprise, banging his head on the sharp metal edge of the hood. He swore, then fell silent, listening for it over the thud of his heart.

There it was again. He looked up to see the wind move through the tops of the pines in a low, sensual moan, not unlike a woman's.

He almost laughed. He hadn't realized how nervous he was. How anxious. Still, it was a damn eerie sound, and as foreign to him as this landscape.

All those miles without seeing another living soul— He felt as disconnected from civilization as if deployed into space. What he wouldn't give right now to see the golden arches of a McDonald's restaurant. Or an interstate. Even a 7-Eleven gas station would perk him up.

He ducked under the car's hood again and quickly made a few adjustments until the engine ran so rough it barely ran at all. Satisfied, he slammed the hood.

Just a few more miles.

As he moved back along the side of the car, he became painfully aware of the darkness just beyond the glow of his headlights. This far north it got dark early and with no lights anywhere other than his head-lamps… His step quickened only slightly, just enough to amuse him as he opened the car door and slid in, closing it firmly behind him. He actually thought about locking his door. This made him laugh.

But it was a short laugh; an oddly sad sound inside the rental car on this lonely stretch of highway just short of hell.

He started to pull back onto the highway. Some-thing caught in his headlights, no bird this time. He threw the car into Reverse, the lights arcing back across the pines, coming to rest on a weathered-white sign standing at a skewed angle in the weeds just yards from where he'd pulled off. Freeze Out Lake. Five miles.

His breath caught as his startled gaze followed the partially obscured dirt tracks in his headlights to the point where the lake road disappeared into the black forest of pines. Not far up there was where the bodies had been found. The gruesome grizzly-bear attack years ago that had made all of the papers. He would never forget the photo of the tent where the grizzly had gone through to drag out the campers inside.

And just last week, Josh Whitaker's car and body had been dragged from the same lake.

His hand actually shook as he shifted into first gear

again. If a place could be cursed, it would be this one. The car engine tried to die. His pulse took off like a shot. For a moment he thought he'd overdone it under the hood, but the car moved forward, the engine still running. Just barely.

Once back on the pavement, he turned on the heater, as if mere heat could chase away the chill. Not a half mile up the highway, it began to rain. Giant, wet drops fell like buckshot, ricocheting off the hood, splattering against the windshield, making the already dark night even blacker.

The next sign he caught in his headlights was: Utopia, Montana.

Home of Charlie Larkin.

He'd expected the town to be small, but not just a few run-down buildings out in the middle of nowhere. If this was their idea of Utopia—

Through the curtain of rain, he spotted the garage first. Could hardly miss anything that big. Or that ugly. Plus, it sat right on the edge of town. And town, what there was of it, was perched on the edge of the highway as if pushed out there by the pines.

The once-red words Larkin & Sons Gas and Garage had faded on the side of the gray metal building. Not exactly an imaginative name, but definitely descriptive. Two ancient-looking gas pumps sat under an overhanging roof next to the gunmetal-gray garage. Several jalopies, stripped clean of parts, rusted under the encroaching trees.

He pulled in under the roof next to a pump. The rain pelted the metal roof loud as a drum. The hand-printed notice on the closest pump read Last Gas for Thirty Miles. He turned off the engine and looked expectantly toward the gas station office, wondering which of the Larkins were working tonight.

Unlike the lamps glowing over the pumps, no light shone in the office. It was empty—and dark—except for the round golden glow of a clock on the wall. Seven-thirty-six.

He hadn't even considered the place might be closed. Not on a Friday night. Especially if it was the last gas for thirty miles.

He looked down the main drag through the rain. A few splashes of neon blurred in the wet darkness. Past that, he could see nothing but more highway and trees.

Swearing under his breath, he turned the key to start the car again, not sure what to do and certainly not where to go. The engine clattered to an uncertain life, ran just long enough to rattle his teeth, then quit. He tried it a couple more times without any luck before he turned off the key and slammed his palm against the steering wheel with an oath. Him and his great plan.

Rain beat on the metal roof and the night felt colder than his last stop beside the highway as he opened his door. He drew up the hood on his jacket, zipping the front closed, as he hustled to the front of the car. He'd just started to pop the hood when he heard music and the clank of tools over the sound of the rain on the roof. Glancing toward the garage, he noticed a sliver of light coming from under the second bay door.

He jogged to the office and found it unlocked. Moving toward the music, he stepped through a side door into a large empty bay. Past it, he could see the source of the light in the second bay.

A single bare bulb glowed under an old beat-up Chevy sedan in the second bay. Country music blasted from a cheap radio on the floor nearby. A pair of western boots were sticking out from under the Chevy.

"Hello!" he called over the radio to the soles of the boots.

From under the Chevy came a grunt and what could have been the word "closed."

He'd come too far to be put off. Not only that, he couldn't very well go out and fix his own car and risk the chance the mechanic would see him. Nor was he willing to give up his plan that easily.

"I need to talk to you about my car!" he called down at the boots, wondering if the small work-boot soles belonged to one of the Larkins. With a whole lot of luck, the feet in them would be Charlie's.

This time he thought he heard the word "Monday" over the racket coming out of the radio and something about "gas" and "cash."

He definitely had no intention of waiting a whole weekend without his car if he could help it. Nor was he about to wait that long to make contact with Charlie. He reached over and turned off the radio. "Hello!"

A loud painful thump was followed by the clatter of a wrench and an oath.

"If you wouldn't mind giving me just a minute of your valuable time," Augustus said sarcastically. This wasn't going anything as he'd planned. But the loud

country music had given him a headache and he'd
had all he could take of being ignored.

An instant later, the mechanic rolled out from the
underbelly of the car on the dolly, forcing Augustus
to step back or be run down.

Silhouetted by only the lamp still under the Chevy,
the short, slightly built mechanic got to his feet without a word and methodically began wiping his hands
on a rag.

Augustus was determined to wait him out. He
could feel the grease monkey giving him the once-
over and was surprised that someone so insignifi-
cantly built could look so arrogant standing there in
dirty, baggy overalls and a baseball cap. At six-two
and a hundred and eighty pounds, Augustus knew he
normally intimidated men twice this one's size.

But if this was Charlie Larkin—

"Look," Augustus said, trying to keep his cool.
He'd been jumpy ever since the turnoff at Freeze Out
Lake. Now he told himself that he was just tired and
impatient. That was true. But he was also a little
spooked, which, under most circumstances, was good.
It gave him an edge.

"My car isn't running," he continued, "it's raining
like hell outside and I've been driving all day and I'm
tired and hungry. If you could just take a quick look
at the engine so I can go find a motel for the night."

The mechanic let out a long-suffering sigh and
slowly reached for the light switch on the pillar next
to him with one hand and the brim of his baseball
cap with the other.

"I'm sure it wouldn't take you any—"

The cap came off in the mechanic's hand as an

overhead fluorescent flickered on, stilling anything else Augustus was going to say. A ponytail of fiery auburn hair tumbled out of the cap and a distinctly female voice said, "You just don't take no for an answer, do you?"

Seldom at a loss for words, Augustus simply stared at her for a beat. In the light, it was obvious she was just a snip of a girl, eighteen tops, the cute little smudge of grease on her chin making her look even more childlike. The baggy overalls she wore seemed to swallow her. "*You're* the mechanic?"

She looked down at the overalls that completely disguised anything feminine about her. "Don't I look like a mechanic?"

Truthfully? No. She looked like a girl wearing her boyfriend's overalls, just fooling around under his car while he went out to get burgers and fries.

She stepped past him and headed for the office, but not before he felt a small rush of excitement. The name stitched in red on the soiled breast pocket of the too-large blue overalls read: Charlie.

He hurriedly trailed after her, not sure where she was going or what she planned to do. "It says Larkin & Sons on the sign," he noted. "I was hoping maybe one of the *Larkins* could look at my car. Maybe you could call one of them? Maybe this…Charlie, whose overalls you're wearing?"

She stopped just inside the office and turned to look at him. "Is that your car parked next to the pump?"

Did she see any other cars out there? He nodded and she pushed open the front door and headed for his car. He followed.

She popped open the hood and, without looking at

him, hollered for him to get in and try to start the engine.

Wondering what this would possibly accomplish, he slid behind the wheel, rolled down his window so he could hear her and turned the key.

The poor engine actually started, running noisily and jerkily, shaking the entire car—until she stuck her head around the open hood and motioned for him to turn it off.

"You drove all the way from—" she leaned over the front of the car to glance at the license plate "—Missoula with the car running like this?" she asked. She had a serious, concentrated expression on her face that made her look a little older.

"It just kept getting worse," he lied, leaning out the window a little so she could hear him over the rain.

Her gaze came back to meet his. He hadn't noticed the color of her eyes until then. They were a rich brown, the same color as the string of freckles that trailed across the bridge of her nose. He couldn't help but wonder exactly what her relationship was with Charlie Larkin.

She continued looking at him as if waiting for him to say something more.

Under other circumstances he might have felt guilty about what he was doing. But he'd made a rule years ago: the end would always justify the means. No exceptions. And in this case, it was personal, so God help Charlie Larkin.

"Won't be able to get it fixed tonight," she said at last, then slammed the hood and turned away from him.

What? He knew it was just a simple matter of adjusting the carburetor. Any mechanic could do it. Obviously she was no more a mechanic than he was and knew a damn sight less about car engines than even he did.

"Leave the key in the office and check back in the morning." She started for the office.

He stared at her back for a moment as she headed for the gas-station office door. "Wait a minute!" He scrambled out of the car and after her. She was already through the office headed for the bay and the vehicle she'd been under when he'd found her. Along the way, she'd put her baseball cap back on, the ponytail tucked up inside it again.

"And what do you expect me to do tonight without a car?" he called to her retreating back. "It's raining! Couldn't you call Charlie to fix my car tonight?"

His words seemed to stop her. She turned around slowly to look at him, tilting her head as if she hadn't quite heard what he'd said.

He rephrased his question, reminding himself this was his own fault. He should never have fiddled with the engine until he was sure Larkin was around to repair it. Now, more than ever, he couldn't go out there, adjust the carburetor and drive off.

"You're sure there's no chance of getting it fixed tonight?" he asked.

"No chance."

He swore silently. Okay. "Is there anywhere in town I could rent a car until mine is repaired?"

She shook her head, giving him a look that said he should have known that after one glance at the town.

''Well, is there somewhere I can stay for the night, a hotel or bed-and-break—''

''Murphy's, about a quarter mile up the road, only place in town.''

''Fine,'' he said, resigned to the quarter-mile walk in the rain. He wasn't about to ask her for a ride and there was no telling when the man who belonged in those overalls would be back. ''You're sure Charlie or one of the Larkins will be able to work on my car in the morning?''

''You can count on it.''

He was.

She turned her back on him again and headed for the old Chevy.

He bit back a curse. ''Don't you at least want me to leave my *name?* It's Augustus T.—''

''Gus,'' she said, cutting him off. ''Got it. Just leave your key on the counter in the office.'' She snapped on the radio as she went by it. A country-western song echoed loudly through the garage.

He could hear her putting away tools as he left and wondered if Charlie Larkin worked tomorrow. Or if it would be one of the other sons or the father who'd be working on his car.

Leaving his key on the counter, he went out to pull his briefcase and bag from the car, glad he traveled light. Then he started down the highway toward the far neon, the rain quickly drenching him to the skin.

He hadn't gone but a few yards when he felt the glare of headlights on his back and the sound of a car braking. It stopped next to him. He bent down in the rain to look in as the driver leaned over to roll down the passenger-side window a crack.

"Need a ride?" asked an elderly man.

The rain alone would have made him accept. "As a matter of fact—"

"Get in. I would imagine you're headed for Maybelle Murphy's, right?" the gray-haired, wizened man asked as Augustus shoved his bag into the back seat and climbed into the front. "Not a night for man nor beast," the driver said as he started back down the highway. "Car trouble, huh?"

It was warm in the car and smelled of pipe tobacco, the kind his father used to use. The man didn't give him a chance to answer.

"Name's Emmett Graham, I run the only mercantile here in town. If you haven't eaten yet, the special at the Pinecone Café tonight is chicken-fried steak. Stays open till ten."

His stomach growled, reminding he hadn't eaten since morning. Emmett didn't seem to notice when he didn't reciprocate and introduce himself. "Sounds like you know the town and probably everyone in it."

"Hell, you've already met half the people here."

Augustus knew the man was exaggerating, but not by much. He was curious about the girl he'd met— and the man whose overalls she'd had on. "Well, you're definitely the friendliest half I've met so far."

The old man nodded with a smile. "Charlie ain't too hospitable at times." He pulled up in front of Murphy's.

Through the rain Augustus could see a short row of small log cabins set in the pines. "I haven't met Charlie yet. I assume he's one of the sons, but if he's anything like the girl I just saw at his garage—"

"Girl?" The old man let out a laugh. "Just goes

to show that you shouldn't believe everything you read. There is no Larkin & *Sons*. Burt and Vera never had any sons. Burt just got all fired up when Vera finally got pregnant. He had a fancy-pants sign painter from Missoula come in and change the name to Larkin & Sons.'' The old man was shaking his head as if this wasn't the first time he'd told this particular story. ''But after Charlotte was born, Vera couldn't have any more kids. Not that a half-dozen sons would have made Burt more proud than his Charlie. He died a happy man, knowing that Charlie would always keep the garage going. She quit college after his heart attack—he just fell over dead one day while working on a car—and Charlie took over running the garage.''

Augustus stared at Emmett, telling himself the old man must be mistaken. That couldn't have been the Charlie Larkin he'd come two thousand miles to find. ''She's just a *girl*.''

The old man smiled. ''Only looks young. She must be twenty-five by now—no, more like twenty-six.'' He looked up at Murphy's blinking neon. ''Shouldn't be a problem getting a bed.'' There were no cars parked in front of any of the cabins. ''Maybelle will see you're taken care of tonight and then Charlie will get your car running in the morning.'' Emmett glanced over at him and must have misread his expression. ''Don't worry, Gus. Charlie is one hell of a mechanic.''

Augustus wouldn't put money on *that*. But he nodded, thanked Emmett and, taking his bag from the back, climbed out. He stood in the rain, hardly feeling it, watching the old man drive away as he realized that Emmett had called him Gus. Only one person in this town even knew his name and she called him Gus.

He felt a chill quake through him that had nothing to do with the rain or the cold as he glanced back down the highway toward Larkin & Sons Gas and Garage.

Charlotte "Charlie" Larkin.

His killer was a woman.

Chapter Two

Charlie Larkin stood in the dark of the office watching the stranger through the rain and night, wondering who he was and why he'd come here. Especially now. More to the point, she wondered why he'd pretended he'd driven the rental car all the way from Missoula with the engine running that badly.

He'd lied about it getting worse. But why? A carburetor just didn't get that out of adjustment. Any decent mechanic would know at once that the engine had been fooled with.

She glanced out at the car. A tan sedan with a Missoula, Montana, license-plate number and a car-rental sticker on the back bumper.

A set of headlights blurred past, the rainy glow changing from a wash of pale yellow to blurred bright red as the car braked. She watched Emmett Graham offer the stranger a ride down to Murphy's, wishing perversely that she hadn't called Emmett and asked him to give the guy a lift. Maybe a walk in the rain would do the man some good. But she knew Emmett would be headed home and that he wouldn't mind

and she didn't have the patience to wait for the man
to walk that far.

She waited until she saw Emmett's car turn off the
highway into Murphy's before she slipped the heavy
wrench into the pocket of her overalls, then picked
up the key from the counter and headed for the rental
car.

No reason to look under the hood again. She didn't
expect any more surprises with the engine, nothing
more to learn there about the man than she already
had.

She opened the driver's-side door and slid in, closing it firmly behind her, feeling vulnerable for those
precious seconds when the dome light illuminated her
through the rain. Now in the dark again, she saw Emmett back out of Murphy's, the right side of his car
empty. The stranger would be checking in. She had
time.

"HOW LONG WILL YOU be staying?" the elderly desk
clerk inquired as she peered at Augustus through the
lines of her trifocals with obvious curiosity. The air
around her reeked of cheap perfume. Gardenia,
maybe. Whatever it was, it made his eyes water.

It seemed Maybelle Murphy had been in a hurry.
Tendrils of bottle-red hair poked out from under a
hastily tied bright floral scarf. Her freshly applied red
lipstick was smeared into the wrinkle lines above her
lips and her cheeks flamed at two high points along
her jawline where she'd slapped on color. She seemed
a little breathless.

He could only assume guests at the motel were so
infrequent they'd become an occasion. He couldn't

imagine that her getting all dolled up had anything to do with him since she'd been behind the desk when he'd entered the office and she couldn't have known he was headed this way since he hadn't known himself until fifteen minutes ago.

She cocked her head at him, making the tarnished brass earrings dangling from her sagging lobes jingle, as she waited for his answer.

How long would he be staying? He'd planned to stay in different hotels as he always did, having found that was the safest—and the most private. But it obviously wasn't going to be an option in Utopia.

"I'm not sure," he admitted, just anxious to get a room, a hot shower, dry clothes, food. Mostly, he needed time to think. About Charlie. He was still shocked she was the one he'd come so far to find.

"It's cheaper by the week," the woman offered sweetly.

It was cheap enough by the day and he doubted this would take a week. "Let's just start with one night."

She nodded. "Car's broke down, huh."

Either news traveled fast or car trouble was the only reason anyone slowed down, let alone stopped, in Utopia.

"Yes, car trouble," he said, sliding his credit card across the worn counter toward her, hoping to hurry her up.

She pushed his card back without even bothering to look at it. "Sorry, we don't do credit."

Of course not. He opened his wallet, took out three tens and handed them to her, putting his credit card away. "I'll need a receipt."

"Oh, so you're here on business, Gus?" the woman said as she counted out his change.

"No, I just like to keep track of my expenses," he snapped, annoyed that, like Charlie and Emmett, she'd called him Gus. Then remembering she hadn't even bothered to glance at his credit card, figured Charlie must have called Maybelle just as she had Emmett.

"Well, you're obviously not a hunter and it's the wrong time of year for a vacation up here, so…" She eyed him closely. "That doesn't leave a whole lot."

Nosy little busybody, wasn't she? "Just passing through," he said coldly and scooped up the room key, catching sight of a newspaper out of the corner of his eye, the headline bannered across the top: Missing Missoula Man Found At Bottom Of Freeze Out Lake. Foul Play Suspected In Doctor's Death.

"If you give me just a minute, I'll have that receipt you asked—"

He tuned Maybelle out as he snatched up the newspaper and quickly skimmed the story. Maybelle put the receipt and room key on the counter. He grabbed up both.

"Now let me show you how to find number five. It's—"

"I can find it," he said, tossing two quarters on the counter for the newspaper and drawing up the hood on his jacket as he pushed his way back out into the rain.

CHARLIE SAT perfectly still in the darkness of the rental car, listening to the rain hammer the metal roof over the pumps, wishing she could get a sense of the man. A different impression of him than the one she'd picked up earlier in the garage.

The car smelled of his aftershave. A scent as masculine and confident as the man himself. She took hold of the wheel and closed her eyes for a moment, searching, as if he'd left something behind she could sense, something that would reassure her.

After a moment, she opened her eyes to the rain and the night, feeling empty and cold inside as she let go of the wheel. She'd been spending a lot of time alone in the dark lately.

Turning on the dome light, she quickly glanced around the car, not surprised to find it immaculate. No personal possessions of any kind. No beverage containers, spilled chips or empty fast-food bags with cold French fries in the bottom. The car looked as clean as when he'd rented it. Too clean for a drive halfway across Montana. He was a man who didn't like leaving anything of himself, she thought as she snapped off the light.

But as she opened the glove compartment, the bulb inside shone on the small fresh smudge of grease on the palm of her right hand. She looked from it to the steering wheel. He'd left more of himself here than he'd thought.

The rental agreement was right where she'd figured he would have forgotten it: folded neatly inside the glove compartment. Augustus T. Riley. He really called himself that? No street address. Instead, a post-office box in Los Angeles. A phone number.

She memorized the numbers, praying she would never need them, then carefully folded the form and put it back exactly as she'd found it. She'd learned that from her father the first time she'd taken an engine apart under his watchful eye. Remembering how you found it, how you took it apart was the key to putting each piece precisely back where it had been.

She closed the glove compartment and sat for a moment, expecting to feel guilty for this invasion of another person's privacy. *Wanting* to feel guilty. She felt nothing. Augustus T. Riley had given up his rights to privacy when he'd brought her his tampered engine to repair. When he'd come looking for Charlie Larkin.

She opened the car door, hit the lock and, pocketing the key, started back toward the office. The rain had slacked off a little and the temperature had dropped. There would be snow on the ground by morning. She glanced up the highway toward Murphy's, wondering where the stranger was now, concerned he was someone she had reason to fear but not knowing why.

She sensed, rather than saw, the furtive movement off to her left. A hooded figure came out of the darkness and the rain, barreling down on her. She half turned, her hand going to the wrench she'd slipped into the pocket of her overalls, stopping just short of the cold steel.

"Wayne," she let out on a relieved breath.

He didn't seem to notice. "Hey, Charlie." As always, he looked embarrassed and apologetic at the same time. "I didn't see you." He took a swipe at his wet face with his sleeve. "Raining pretty hard." He seemed to focus on her, his eyes always a little too bright. "I hope I didn't keep you past your dinner."

She shook her head and smiled her half smile. Friendly, but not too. "You know I stay open until nine on Friday nights."

He nodded vigorously, obviously not knowing anything of the kind. She'd always closed early this time of year, and with everything that had been going on lately, she'd shortened the gas station hours even more.

"I got your car running," she said as she led the way inside.

He pulled back his hood, throwing off a spray of rainwater as he trotted to keep up. "It's a good old car."

He always said that. She'd given up telling him he should look for something with a few less miles on it. She understood the sentimental value of a car, even one as bad-looking as this old Chevy. Wayne's dad, Ted, had given him the Chevy when Wayne was seventeen—just before Ted had died. That had been five years ago, five years of trying to keep the old car running.

Water dripped from the dingy cap Wayne wore under the hood as he dug deep into his worn jeans and pulled out two crumpled bills. Charlie watched him smooth one of them across his thigh, his curly blond head bent with such concentration it hurt to watch him.

"I get paid next Friday if this isn't enough," Wayne said, working the wrinkles out of the second twenty. He sacked and stocked groceries and supplies at Emmett Graham's small market.

"Actually, you could do me a favor," Charlie said, looking at the old Chevy rather than at Wayne. "I

heard your mother raised more winter squash than she
could use this year. You could save me a trip and get
me some in payment. Otherwise, I'm just going to
have to drive over and buy them from her.''

Wayne looked up, both the surprise and confusion
only momentary since this was how their conversations over the bill went every time. ''Squash?''

''Aunt Selma has her heart set on winter squash for
Sunday dinner.''

Wayne nodded vigorously. ''Mom's got lotsa
squash.''

''Great.'' She handed him the keys to the Chevy
and touched the garage-door opener. The overhead
rose slowly with a groan, letting in the wet and cold
and dark. Just beyond the door, she could see puddles,
night slick, but no rain dimpling the surface. Snow
fell silent as death.

''I'll get the squash and bring them right away,''
Wayne said excitedly as he opened his car door.

Charlie started to tell him to wait till morning, but
caught herself. Wayne would be back in a few
minutes and she didn't want him worrying himself all
night about paying his bill. ''That would be great.''

He drove off, hitting all of the puddles, reminding
her he was part kid, part man, caught for this lifetime
somewhere in between.

She started to close the bay door, then remembered
the rental car. She still had the key in her pocket.

The interior smelled of Gus, even over all the others who had rented the car. Odd, she thought. A man
who gave little away about himself and yet invaded
whatever space he occupied—and didn't give it up
easily. A dangerous man.

She coaxed the engine to run long enough to get the car into the bay, hurriedly closing the overhead door behind it, feeling vulnerable again, as if she'd let in more than she knew, more than she could handle.

At the sound of Wayne's old Chevy, she turned out the lights, left the rental car key on the counter in the office and stepped outside to find that he'd brought her two large boxes of produce, including apples and pumpkins. She helped him load the boxes into her van parked on the side of the building. Then watched him drive off before she went back in to lock up for the night.

Just inside the office, she stopped, chilled at the sight of the rental car in the second far bay—a small faint light glowing inside it.

The chill deepened as a knife of fear cut up her spine. She hadn't left a light on inside the car. That she was sure of. She stood in the doorway, heart pounding so loudly she couldn't hear over it. She breathed deeply, trying to still the cold dread as she caught the scent of Augustus T. Riley's aftershave over the deep-seated smell of motor oil and cleaner. *He was here.*

Blindly, she reached for the overhead light switch, her free hand going to the wrench in her overalls even as common sense told her it wasn't much of a weapon.

The fluorescents came on, illuminating both bays. He wasn't here.

But he had *been.*

She turned to look back at the counter. The key to the rental car was gone.

She moved slowly across the cold concrete to the car. Even from a distance she could see that the glove compartment was open, the small bulb illuminating one dark corner of the car—and the garage.

Walking around to the passenger side, she opened the door, not surprised he'd left the key in the ignition. He'd wanted her to know that he'd been here. *Because he'd left her something.*

The clipping had been torn from the newspaper, the edges ragged, the paper still damp from the storm. He'd left it where she couldn't miss the headline: Missing Missoula Man Found At Bottom Of Freeze Out Lake. Foul Play Suspected In Doctor's Death.

Chapter Three

Augustus brushed fresh snow from his jacket as he stepped through the door into the Pinecone Café. He should have been freezing cold. He definitely was wet, first from the rain, then the snow. Obviously, he wasn't prepared for this kind of weather, but he didn't care. He was on the chase—and he loved nothing better.

A hush fell over the café as everyone turned to look at who'd come through the door. He shrugged out of his lightweight jacket, realizing his dress shirt and slacks made him conspicuous enough, but now they were wet. He could feel all eyes on him. Forget anonymity in Utopia, he thought as he hung the jacket next to five tan canvas coats in various sizes, styles and stages of decline.

Feeling as if he was on center stage, he turned slowly to take in the café—and its customers. The Pinecone was just a hole-in-the-wall with three booths and a half-dozen stools along a worn counter that faced the grill. A middle-aged couple sat in the first booth, two men in the next, the third empty.

At the counter, an elderly woman knitted, her large

bag on the stool next to her. A middle-aged woman
in a waitress uniform and nurse's shoes stood across
the counter from her smoking a cigarette, looking as
if she owned the place. At the far end of the counter,
a lone man sat bent over his coffee. He didn't look
up.

"Good evening," Augustus said to the curious
faces.

"Evenin'," the woman behind the counter replied.
All except the guy at the counter gave him a nod, the
women a polite smile as he worked his way past them
to the empty booth. Friendly little place, wasn't it?

He slid in, his back to the wall so he could watch
the door, an old habit.

Conversations resumed. The two men in the next
booth talking about a tractor that the one named
Leroy couldn't get to run. The middle-aged couple
eating in silence, a sure sign they were married, and
at the counter, the older waitress chatting with the
knitter about a sweater she'd started for her granddaughter. The lone twenty-something man seemingly
in his own world.

"Hi!" A perky young bottled blonde in a too-tight
uniform came out of the kitchen to slide a plastic-
covered menu across the table at him. "Our special
is chicken-fried steak. Comes with soup, salad,
mashed potatoes, gravy, peas, a roll and dessert for
six-fifty."

Amazing. "Sold," he said, smiling as he slid the
menu back at her without opening it. She looked to
be in her late twenties, about Charlotte "Charlie"
Larkin's age, if Emmett was to be believed, and she

was a hell of a lot friendlier, both things Augustus hoped to use to his advantage.

She gave him the full effect of her smile. "Can I get you some coffee?"

"I'd love a cup. It's a little damp out there."

She laughed at that, considering he was soaked to the skin and wearing the least appropriate clothing possible. Everyone else in the place had on jeans or those tan canvas pants that seemed to be so popular in this town along with flannel shirts and winter boots.

"It's going to get a whole lot damper," she said, coming back with the coffeepot and a cup. She poured him some and said, "Supposed to drop a good eight inches of snow before morning."

Just what he needed. He'd have to buy a coat and boots. Fortunately he'd had the sense to bring a pair of jeans. "Isn't it too early in the year?"

She laughed. "This is Montana. It can snow any month—and has." She left and came back with a bowl of steaming vegetable soup. It smelled wonderful and tasted even better.

He ate his soup quickly, needing the warmth and hungrier than he'd been for a while. His clothes were starting to dry out, and while he was more comfortable, some of his earlier elation was starting to wear off and he wasn't sure why. He suspected it was because Charlie Larkin wasn't at all what he'd expected—and not just because she was female. He'd known his share of female killers and knew that they came in all sizes and shapes. Some were even as cute and innocent-looking as Charlie.

No, something else about her bothered him and he couldn't put his finger on it.

He blamed his sudden uneasiness on the fact that, while what evidence there was pointed to Charlie Larkin—it was only circumstantial. Nor was this the way he normally operated. All the other times, he'd come in after the arrest had been made, after the killer was behind bars—or out on bail. This time he was going after the murderer himself. This time, it was personal.

Taking a sip of his coffee, he reassured himself that he was dead-on with this case. What evidence there was had led him straight to Charlie Larkin—and his gut instincts hardly ever let him down. Except for that one time, which he tried not to dwell on.

But that one mistake had taught him well. He'd trusted one of his subjects and it had almost cost him his life—and his career. That's why he would never let himself get emotionally involved with a suspect, again.

Not that there was any chance of that with this case, he thought, remembering the churlish young woman in the baggy overalls he'd met at the garage. So at odds with her angel-cute face, the freckles, the big brown eyes, framed by all that dark-flame hair. Oh, yeah, he could see how a woman with her looks and spunk would be like honey to bears to most men.

But he wasn't most men. So what was it about Charlie Larkin that had him worried? Something about her reminded him of Natalie. The thought shook him to his core. He glanced out the window, feeling too isolated, too ill-prepared for the weather— and this dinky little town. How was he going to be able to accomplish anything without even rudimentary services? He'd tried to make a call from his motel room, which—big surprise—had no phone and he got no service on his cell phone.

He'd seen two pay phones so far, one tacked on the wall a few feet inside the café door and a primitive-looking one outside Larkin's. Neither exactly private. And the one was out in the weather and way too close to Charlie Larkin.

The conversation at the all-male booth had changed to the price of lumber and those damn tree huggers who were ruining the logging industry.

The woman in the waitress uniform put out her cigarette. "So, Leroy, did I hear you're still trying to get that old tractor running?" she inquired of the suspender-wearing man in the booth. She had a face with a lot of miles on it and a voice gravelly from smoking.

"Got to, Helen. Can't afford a new one. Goin' to have to plow snow with it pretty darned soon. Maybe Charlie'll have a look at it when she gets the time," he said, wagging his head.

Helen, who no doubt was the café's owner, looked over in Augustus's direction. "Get settled in at Murphy's, Gus?"

Gus. It wasn't bad enough that Charlie Larkin had told everyone in town about him, she hadn't even gotten his name right. "It's Augustus," he said and gave Helen a smile to soften it. "Augustus T. Riley."

She chuckled as if he'd said something funny, obviously not recognizing the name. "Well, welcome to Utopia. You're the big news of the day."

"Slow news day, huh," he said, seeing an opening. "I would think that fellow who got pulled out of the lake would still be news."

"Shoot, that was over a week ago. Old news now

and not the kind we like to be known for.'' She stepped back into the kitchen and proceeded to finish up some cooking she had going on. ''Trudi, your orders are up.''

He wondered what kind of news Utopia liked being known for.

''Here ya go, T.J.,'' Trudi said cheerfully as she slid a plateful of food across the counter to the guy sitting alone. She wasted a big smile on him. He didn't even bother to look up at her, just grunted something Augustus couldn't hear.

Trudi stood there for a moment, then went to deliver a couple of burgers to Leroy's table and brought Augustus his salad. ''Was creepy though, you know, if you think that his body was in the lake all this time,'' she said, picking up the thread of the earlier conversation.

''Since last fall,'' he agreed, trying not to think about it. ''So, did you know him?''

She shook her head. ''He wasn't from around here.''

Augustus knew that. Josh Whitaker had been an emergency-room doctor in Missoula at the hospital. He was thirty-four, two years younger than Augustus, single and lived with two other residents in a large house near the hospital. His death was being investigated as possible foul play after the coroner reported Josh had been hit in the back of the head with a blunt object, his car then pushed into the lake where it sank from view.

No one knew what Josh Whitaker was doing in Utopia, thirty miles from the nearest real town. In this part of Montana, that thirty miles felt like three hundred. Augustus had never felt such isolation and couldn't imagine why Josh had come up here all the way from Missoula. Josh had been missing for almost a year, his body finally discovered in late September by two local teenagers, just before the cold spell.

But what Augustus knew that the press didn't, according to phone company records, was that Josh had received two phones calls from Utopia just before he disappeared. Both from the pay phone outside Larkin & Sons Gas and Garage. He'd almost placed several phone calls to that pay phone, along with another to a C. Larkin that same day, the call to C. Larkin less than a minute in length, making Augustus wonder if Josh had reached Charlie. Her name had also showed up in an old date book of Josh's with a notation beside it: help line.

What Augustus needed was to find out what Charlotte "Charlie" Larkin's relationship had been with Josh Whitaker, how they'd met no doubt through Josh's statewide help line program, why Josh might have come to Utopia to see her and why she might want him dead. No small task.

But hadn't Emmett mentioned that Charlie Larkin had to quit college when her father had his heart attack? Was it possible she and Josh had met while she was attending the University of Montana in Missoula? That was where Josh had started his first help line.

"What a terrible way to die," Trudi was saying. "Drowning." She shivered.

"I heard it's not that bad, like going to sleep," the knitting woman said.

"Marcella, I think you're confusing drowning with hypothermia," Helen said.

"Starvation," Leroy said. "I guess that or a quick heart attack is the way to go."

"Beats putting a gun to your head," Helen agreed.

An argument ensued over what caliber gun worked best. Augustus tried to steer the conversation back to the body in the lake. "Do they know what the drowned guy was doing here?"

The customers looked to Helen as if anyone in town would know, it would be her. She shrugged.

"Isn't this lake off the beaten path?" Augustus asked.

"Yeah, but maybe he'd heard about those campers that were eaten by that grizzly and wanted to see the place," Trudi said, all big-eyed.

Helen grimaced. "That's pretty morbid and it was years ago. I can't imagine he would have even heard about it."

Augustus remembered from the national news stories when he was a senior in high school and working on the school newspaper. Mostly he remembered because there were only a few things that ate you. Sharks. Gators. Grizzlies. "Didn't I read in the paper that he was seeing a local woman?" he lied, drawing the conversation back to Josh Whitaker.

"Wouldn't know anything about that," Helen said, going back to the kitchen to check on his chicken-fried steak. A few minutes later she handed Trudi a huge plate overflowing with meat, gravy and mashed potatoes and a side of canned peas through the pass-through.

"Charlie fixing your car, huh?" Helen asked him, returning to her spot at the counter across from Marcella.

"In the morning," he said, taking the opening. "I heard she's a pretty good mechanic."

"Best in five counties," Helen boasted as she lit another cigarette, definitely at home with the place, with herself.

Best in thirty miles, he could buy. Five counties though? That he seriously doubted.

"If anyone can get your car running, it's Charlie," Leroy agreed.

Anyone with even a little mechanical training could get his car running, if they wanted to. And if Charlie Larkin was as good as everyone in this town claimed, she would know that. The thought disturbed him.

"Yep, they don't come any better than Charlie," Helen agreed. "I wouldn't be surprised if she was over there right now working on your car."

He wouldn't put money on that.

"Like that time she found that family broke down outside of town," Marcella said, knitting as she talked. "Remember that bunch? Must have had a dozen kids in that old motor home. Charlie took them food and got the rig running, though heaven only knows how."

Helen was nodding, obviously savoring the story. "They didn't have two nickels to rub together, had spent all their money on gas trying to get to the coast—and a job the father said he had waiting for him. Sounded like a story to me, but you know Charlie."

He didn't. But he sure wanted to. He took a bite of the steak. It was delicious.

"Charlie told him he could pay his bill after he got settled." Helen shook her head. "I would have sworn she'd never see a dime of that money, but a year later she gets a check—with interest. Don't that beat all?''

''That's one hell of a story,'' Augustus agreed, wondering how much of it was now Utopia legend and how much of it was true.

''Oh, we could go on all night about Charlie,'' Helen said.

''Like the way she's helped Earlene with that baby,'' Marcella said. She glanced back at Augustus. ''Earlene's a single mother. The baby's father's dead.''

Charlie Larkin sounded like a saint. He'd found out a long time ago, though, that the nicest, most charitable person in the world was still capable of committing murder. But it certainly made him all the more curious about Charlie. And all the more determined to get her.

The twenty-something man at the counter Trudi had called T.J. suddenly pushed his half-full plate back, slapped down some bills on the counter and stalked out, grabbing his coat before disappearing through the door without a word.

''Who was that?'' Augustus asked Trudi quietly when she came over to his table to refill his coffee cup.

She glanced toward the closing door. ''Oh, that's just T. J. Blue.''

''He seemed upset.''

''He's always upset when Charlie Larkin's name comes up,'' she whispered and then went off with the coffeepot to refill cups.

Upset when Charlie Larkin's name came up, was he? Augustus made a point of reminding himself to have a talk with this T. J. Blue who hadn't said a word when Helen and everyone else were going on about the virtues of Charlie Larkin. Interesting.

"Emmett told me that Charlie had to come home from college early and take over the garage after her father's heart attack," Augustus said to Helen who was clearing away T. J. Blue's dishes after his abrupt departure.

Helen nodded, but said nothing, as if he was on the verge of asking too many questions.

"She worked in the garage alongside her father every summer," Leroy said. "Burt insisted she get an education although everyone in town knew he hoped she'd come home and work with him after she graduated."

"What was she majoring in at Missoula before she had to quit?" he asked casually, taking a bite of his steak. It could have been cardboard for all the attention he paid it as he waited for someone to confirm his theory that Charlie Larkin had gone to college in the same town Josh Whitaker was a doctor.

Helen frowned, looking suspicious.

"Business, wasn't it, Helen?" Marcella asked, looking up from her knitting. "But she didn't go to school in Missoula. She went to Bozeman." Miles apart.

"I thought Emmett told me—never mind," Augustus said. "I must have heard wrong." So how had they met?

Charlie had to be the reason Josh Whitaker had come to Utopia and ended up in Freeze Out Lake last fall. Augustus would stake his reputation on it. But what was their connection? The obvious female-male one? Or something else?

A thought struck him like a brick. The use of the pay phone at the garage—rather than her home phone. "Charlie isn't married, is she?"

Helen studied him for a long moment. "No." Her gaze said he'd just asked too many questions.

"She sounds like someone I'd like to get to know better." He shrugged and grinned his you-know-us-guys grin.

Helen seemed to relax a little. She obviously knew how men could be. She went around the counter to sit next to Marcella and proceeded to tell her about some yarn she'd found on sale in Missoula.

"Got all that firewood split and stacked yet for winter?" Leroy asked the man across from him.

"See ya, Helen," the woman in the first booth said as she and her husband left, leaving money on the table.

"Take care, Kate. You, too, Bud."

Augustus concentrated on his food, listening to the conversations move from one mundane topic to the next. No one paid him any attention. He must be old news.

But he saw Trudi watching him when she thought he wasn't looking and he knew, the way he always knew, that here was someone who had something she was dying to tell him.

The chase always made him ravenous and this one was no exception. It wouldn't be easy with most of the town trying to convince him Charlie Larkin was a saint. But at least one person in town wasn't wild about Charlie: T. J. Blue. And Augustus had a feeling he'd find more. He smiled and dug into his dinner.

HE'D EATEN all he could and shoved his plate away when Trudi came over to his booth. She was all business, making a project out of writing up his bill, then taking his napkin to write something on it before sliding it and the bill under the edge of his saucer. She refilled his cup with coffee he'd just said he didn't want. She seemed nervous.

He could feel Helen's gaze on them, watching eagle-eyed, and Trudi must have felt it, too. She hurriedly cleared up his dishes, everything but his coffee, and disappeared back into the kitchen again.

He stared after her for a moment, then plucked the bill and napkin from under the edge of the saucer. Along with the six dollars and fifty cents he owed for dinner, she'd written on his napkin: "I get off at ten."

He glanced at his watch. That would give him time to get ready for her. He pulled out his pen and wrote, Murphy's, No. 5 on the napkin, then dropped a ten on top of the bill. With luck Trudi had something good to offer him.

As he left the café, Helen called after him, "See ya, Gus." He could feel her watching as he walked past the front window of the café. He wondered how long it would take her to call Charlie Larkin and tell her he'd been asking personal questions about her. The thought pleased him, since he'd only just begun.

I'm coming for you, Charlie.

Chapter Four

Charlie pushed through the kitchen door of the old farmhouse she shared with her mother and aunt, a huge box of produce in her arms.

"Let me guess. Wayne Dreyer's old Chevy broke down again." Aunt Selma shook her freshly-permed, gray head as she walked over to the table to peer inside the box Charlie set down. Her aunt looked small and frail next to the huge box, older somehow.

"I've got another one in the van," Charlie said and went back out to get it through the falling snow, thick as cotton ticking, the old farmhouse and the surrounding trees a blur of white.

Her aunt was giving her that look when she came back in.

"Winter squash, apples and pumpkins," Charlie said, sliding the second huge box onto the table next to the first.

"I can see that," Selma said. "There's enough squash alone to last three winters. And pumpkins— Land-sakes, what will we do with all of them? You'd better hope that boy's car doesn't break down again until berry season."

"He got the idea that we eat a lot of pumpkin pie," she said, shrugging out of her coat. This time last year the water pump had gone on Wayne's Chevy and she'd taken pumpkins as payment, going on about her Aunt Selma's need for fresh pumpkin for her pies.

Her aunt shook her head. "You remind me of your father."

"Thank you," Charlie said, going to hang her coat on the hook by the back door.

"That wasn't a compliment."

Charlie turned to smile at her.

Her aunt's gaze softened. "Is anything wrong?"

"No."

Selma waved that off. "I know you, girl," she said, frowning. "Something's happened."

Some people in town said Selma had The Gift, that she could practically look into your head and see things that no one else could—including the future.

There had been times when Charlie wasn't so sure they weren't right. But mostly she believed her aunt just paid more attention to the little things, things other people maybe didn't take the time to notice. Not that it wasn't damn eerie on occasion. And a real pain if you preferred to keep your problems to yourself.

The phone rang. Charlie tried to hide her relief as she gave her aunt a shrug and picked up the receiver from the wall phone.

"That guy whose car broke down—Gus—he just left," Helen whispered. "I thought you'd want to know."

"Really?" she said and smiled at her aunt, knowing there was more.

"He was asking a lot of questions."

"About what?" she asked, trying to keep her voice light.

"About that man who drowned in the lake and about you."

Charlie let out a little laugh and turned away from her aunt. "Well, you know what they say about curiosity."

"That's not the worst part," Helen said. "Trudi warmed right up to him. You know how she is."

Everyone knew how Trudi Murphy was. The stranger probably would know soon enough.

"I think you should try to find out something about him," Helen said. "I don't like the looks of him." She didn't like the looks of most men. Blame it on four bad marriages and a weakness for losers. "What's he wanting to know about you for anyway?"

"I don't know, but I'm sure it's nothing." She wished that were true.

"I hope you're right," Helen said. "Once his car is fixed, maybe he'll leave. Maybelle said he only paid for one night."

"That's good." But she had a feeling it didn't mean a thing. "Thanks for letting me know." She hung up and turned, feeling her aunt's intent gaze.

"Charlotte—" Selma began.

"What in the world?" her mother said from the doorway. Vera's eyes widened with wonder, as if the boxes on the table were brightly wrapped presents instead of vegetables from the gourd family and the fruit that destroyed Eden.

Her mother was smaller than Selma and lacked her sister's strength. Vera had always been the fragile one, her pale skin almost translucent, her hair now downy feather white.

Aunt Selma gave Charlie a warning look, one she knew only too well. *Don't upset your mother.* The words should have been stitched on their living-room pillows.

"I've been wanting to make some pumpkin pies," Selma said.

Vera Larkin smiled dreamily. Her cardigan sweater had fallen off one shoulder. "I do love pumpkin pie. With ice cream." She frowned. "Or is it whipped cream?"

"Either sounds good," Selma told her as she pulled her sister's sweater around her thin shoulders.

Charlie noticed that her mother's slippers were on the wrong feet as she watched the two leave the room. She closed her eyes, the pain too intense. It broke her heart to see her mother like this and growing worse each day.

If it wasn't for Aunt Selma... It was hard to believe that Selma was almost seventy, the older of the sisters. She'd never married. When Charlie was a child, she'd found a yellowed wedding dress in the attic. Her mother had told her a romantic story about Selma falling wildly in love with a soldier. They were to be married, but just days before he was coming home, his plane was shot down. Devastated, Selma had sworn never to love another man.

Of course, there were people in Utopia who swore the story was as phony as Trudi Murphy's bust. But then how did Charlie explain the wedding dress still in the attic? If Selma's "sight" was to be believed, maybe Selma had known long ago that Vera was going to need her and that's why she'd never married. Maybe Selma had called off the wedding after another one of Vera's miscarriages had laid her up. It would be like Selma.

Vera had never been strong, according to Selma. She'd married Burt at eighteen full of hope, but quickly became weakened both physically and spiritually by miscarriages and disappointments, until finally Charlie was born. Vera was almost forty by then.

Just twenty-one years later, she lost Burt to a heart attack. It had been a blow that had left her mother crippled emotionally and brought Charlie racing back from college to take over the garage. That had been four years ago. Aunt Selma had been there, though, each time Vera needed her. It wasn't surprising that Selma had been the one to notice Vera's Alzheimer's first.

"Are you warm enough?" Selma was asking Vera in the living room. "It's snowing out. Maybe I should throw more logs on the fire. Would you like that?" Selma glanced over her shoulder as she helped Vera into a wingback chair in front of the fireplace, her look clear: *We will talk later.*

Charlie had no doubt of that. Selma and Vera had already eaten dinner. Charlie could smell the chicken and dumplings Selma had saved her. There was a warm apple pie, too.

Charlie had tried to get Selma to slow down.

"Cooking and caring for my sister is what I've always done," Selma had snapped. "Let me enjoy myself and don't get in my way." She'd softened the words with a smile. "You know how much I love doing this."

Charlie had nodded and stayed out of her way, helping out as much as she could behind the scenes.

While Charlie ate, Vera chattered away about things that had happened forty years ago. Selma was too quiet, as if she could read Charlie's thoughts, which kept returning to the stranger in town.

After dinner and dishes, Charlie got her coat from the peg and went out on the porch, hoping the cold night air would clear her head. It wasn't long before she heard the soft creak of slipper steps on the floorboards behind her.

"Well?" Selma's voice sounded hoarse with worry.

She didn't turn around. "It's nothing." She tried to sound unconcerned.

"Then why do you seem…scared?"

Scared? Is that what this was? This quaking inside her. This high-frequency jitter, like being connected to a high-voltage battery all the time. She wouldn't have been surprised if she started throwing off sparks. At first it had been a low buzz. Almost a nervous energy. Anxiety. Worry. But now she vibrated with what had to be more than fear. She hugged herself as if that would still her terror. At least long enough to reassure her aunt.

"There's something I need to ask you." Selma seemed to hesitate. "Does this have anything to do with that young man they pulled from the lake?"

Charlie turned slowly to look at her aunt. Selma stood in a pool of light from the kitchen window wearing a thick wool sweater over her polyester pantsuit. Charlie remembered her mother secretly knitting the sweater several years ago. A Christmas present in Selma's favorite colors, browns, golds and reds.

Even from here Charlie could see the mistakes in the pattern. The signs had been there that long ago, only Charlie hadn't recognized them. But then, it was so hard to admit that someone you loved was losing her mind.

"Yes," Charlie said. It had everything to do with Josh Whitaker.

Selma reached for the porch railing and closed her eyes, her bare hand pale and bony, veins blue against the white skin, frail.

Charlie started to reach for her, afraid her aunt was going to collapse. But she drew back her hand at the last minute as Selma's eyes snapped open.

Before she saw the tears, Charlie was going to tell her aunt everything. The weight of holding something like this inside just seemed too much to bear alone any longer. But the tears stopped her. Selma had always been strong, but this was too much of a burden for anyone, especially someone you loved.

"I'm just upset because the death reminds me of when Quinn was killed," Charlie said quickly.

The relief in Selma's expression was worth the half lie Charlie had had to tell.

"You still think about Quinn Simonson?" her aunt asked, sounding surprised but stronger. "That was so long ago and I didn't think your relationship with him was that serious."

Charlie shook her head. "No, but he was my *first* boyfriend."

"The Simonsons aren't giving you a hard time

again, are they?'' Selma demanded fiercely, reminding Charlie of a bantam rooster. ''Those people. They
just want to blame someone for their golden boy's
death and you're an easy target.''

Golden boy only fit Quinn because of his blond
good looks and because Phil and Norma Simonson
had put him on a pedestal above even their oldest son,
Forest. To them, Quinn could do no wrong. Unfortunately, Charlie knew better.

''It's not the Simonsons,'' Charlie said. ''This latest accident at the lake just brings back all the awful
memories from before.'' Not that the Simonsons had
let her forget for a moment over the past seven years
what they believed she'd done—killed their son.

''I'm so sorry this had to happen now,'' Selma
said. ''You have enough to concern yourself with.''

''I'm fine.'' She hugged Selma, tears springing to
her eyes at the frailty she felt in her aunt's wiry-thin
frame.

''Oh, Charlie.'' Her aunt brushed a dry kiss across
her cheek. ''You have taken on so much with your
mother and me.''

''That's not true,'' she said. ''You and Mom have
always taken care of me and now you have Mom to
take care of as well.''

Her aunt pulled her sweater around herself, her expression unconvinced. How much did she know? Or
did she just *suspect* the truth?

''It's cold out here,'' Charlie said. ''You should get
back in before Mom misses you.'' She knew that,
more than the cold, would get her aunt back inside,
keep her aunt from asking any more questions.

With obvious reluctance, Selma scuffled back into the house without another word.

Charlie turned to look out at the snow, filled with relief—and regret. The snow had begun to stick and pile up. The way a lot of things in life tended to pile up. When Josh's body was pulled from the lake, she'd felt paralyzed with fear. She hadn't known he was in town. Still didn't understand what could have brought him up here considering that she hadn't seen or spoken to him in four years.

She shook her head, the horror of his murder almost more than she could bear. She closed her eyes. She had just let things happen and now she'd have to pay the price. But she wouldn't make that mistake again. She had to protect her family, no matter what it took.

From somewhere out in the snowy darkness came a low growl. Charlie moved down the porch toward the sound, trying to see the dog through the falling snow. Spark Plug, the name her father had given the puppy just before his death, growled again, this time the growl lower, more serious.

Something was out there. Someone. Charlie felt the soft hair on her neck stand up. Moving silently, she retraced her footsteps and opened the back door. The shotgun was high up on the top shelf, out of her mother's reach—even with a chair. Charlie pulled it down and dug out two buckshot shells from the kitchen drawer. She loaded the gun and stepped back out onto the porch.

By now, snow blanketed the yard and fell in a wall of white. She stood in the dark under the porch roof, staring out into the snowfall. Who was it she had to

fear? Augustus T. Riley. What was he anyway? A
cop? A private investigator hired by Josh's family?
Did it matter?

Spark Plug growled again, only this time farther
away, then began to bark. Past the barking, Charlie
heard an engine turn deep in the pines somewhere on
the county road. It sounded like a pickup with a bad
muffler, one of a half dozen around town.

Spark Plug quit barking and after a few minutes
wandered out of the snowstorm. He was a true mutt,
shortlegged, with a spotted white, brown and black
short-haired coat and big floppy ears. When he saw
her, he wagged his stubby tail and climbed up the
steps to the porch.

Charlie put the shotgun aside to brush snow from
the dog's back. She waited until the sound of the
truck died away, then she took him inside where Aunt
Selma pretended to scold him softly for not coming
home sooner for dinner.

"Spark Plug barking at another coyote?" Selma
asked as Charlie returned the shotgun to the top shelf
and the shells to the kitchen drawer.

"Sure seems that way." Charlie took her time cutting three pieces of apple pie, thinking about the truck
she'd heard leaving and Spark Plug's worried growl.

Then she took the plates of pie into the living
room where her mother was surprised all over again
to see her.

Chapter Five

Augustus heard the tap at his door just after ten. He'd give Trudi one thing, she hadn't wasted any time.

He took one quick glance around the cabin to make sure he hadn't left anything important lying around—like his notebook. The cabin was straight out of an old Western. Knotty-pine walls, horse-motif bedspread, antler lamp and lonesome-cowboy painting on the wall. Hee-haw!

No one back in L.A. would believe a town like this still existed. He hardly believed it himself.

She knocked again, this time more insistent. Anxious, wasn't she? He doubted it was his charm. Some people took a malicious delight in dishing dirt about other people. As ugly as that trait was, it sure made his job a lot easier.

He swung the door open.

She stood on the tiny porch in an unbuttoned long camel-colored wool coat over a short, low-cut dress and black boots. She bit nervously at her lower lip as she shot periodic glances behind her.

"Hey," he said, a little surprised by the way she was dressed. Even more so by the suspicious way she was acting. Did she think she'd been followed? Or was she just afraid someone would see her coming here? Why was that? "Jealous boyfriend?"

She swung around, obviously startled, and quickly smiled. "I don't have a boyfriend. I mean not a steady one. I like my freedom," she said all coy.

He wished there was another way to get what he needed from her. Obviously she had something different in mind than he did. He leaned against the doorjamb, not wanting to ask her in but knowing that if he didn't he might never know what she was dying to tell him. But at what price?

The snow had stopped falling, the ground glittering cold and white behind her. And just when he thought Utopia couldn't be any more alien to him.

Reluctantly, he stepped aside. "Come on in." As he started to close the door, he looked out in the snowy darkness to see a pickup slow as it passed on the highway. The truck was a dark color, loud—and while he couldn't see more than a silhouette behind the wheel, it was obvious the driver had been looking this way. Looking for Trudi? Or him? The pickup sped up and on past, kicking up snow.

He closed the door and turned to find Trudi sitting on the end of his bed, her coat off, legs crossed, exposing a lot of skin. The little flowered dress was even skimpier than he'd thought.

Sometimes he hated the things he had to do to get what he wanted. But all that mattered was the end result, right? Right. "Can I offer you something to drink?" he asked. "I'm afraid all I have are plastic glasses and tap water."

She smiled and reached into the pocket of her coat,

pulling out a bottle of beer. She handed it to him and dug out another from the other pocket. "I hope you like Moose Drool."

He glanced at the beer. "Who could pass up a beer with such an appealing name."

She laughed at that. In fact, she laughed at everything he said. It made this a whole lot harder.

He pulled out the straight-back chair from the small oak desk. "Are you old enough to drink alcohol?" he asked, straddling the chair to rest his arms on the back.

She gave him an "oh-you-tease" look and took a sip of her beer. "I'm twenty-six."

Charlie's age? "So you must have gone to school with Charlie Larkin."

She nodded and glanced around the cabin. It wasn't that interesting. Then her gaze settled on him. She wet her lips and gave him a come-hither smile. "Is that the only reason you asked me here? To talk about Charlie?"

He must be getting old, because he just wasn't up to this game tonight. He cut to the chase, unable to bear dragging it out any longer. "I got the impression at the café that there was something you wanted to tell me about her."

She seemed startled and suddenly ill at ease. "I can't imagine what it could have been."

He watched her dig at the beer label with her thumbnail. "Give it a little thought, I'll bet it will come to you."

Her eyes narrowed. "Are you a cop or something?"

"Something." Giving her his backup story would

be a waste of a good lie. And there seemed little reason to tell her the truth since it would be out soon enough.

She took a drink of her beer, eyeing him over the bottle. "What's in it for me?"

Finally, solid ground. "Depends on if I find the information of value." When she didn't bother to nail him down on a price, it became apparent she wasn't in it for the money—just as he'd originally suspected.

She sat up straighter on the bed. "You were asking about the guy they found in the lake."

He said nothing.

"He wasn't the first, you know."

His heart kicked up a beat. "First to what?"

"End up dead at the lake. Quinn Simonson was killed leaving Freeze Out Lake right after high-school graduation. His car went off the road."

Augustus shook his head. "What does that have to do with—"

"Quinn was Charlie Larkin's high-school boyfriend. She was there that night. They had a big fight and—"

"What about?"

"Earlene Kurtz. Charlie found out that Earlene was four months pregnant with Quinn's baby." Augustus wondered if Trudi hadn't helped Charlie find out about the pregnancy. He let out a low whistle. "Charlie was mad?"

Trudi snorted. "She was furious. She refused to get back in the car with Quinn even though he promised to take her straight home. He was pretty upset about everyone knowing about Earlene and the pregnancy.

He left and crashed his car on a curve coming off the mountain.''

"Right, so I don't see—"

"Charlie did something to the car."

He took a breath. "Like what?"

She shrugged. "Something to make it crash. She'd just worked on his car the day before the accident— and that night at the lake, she was over by it just before he left."

He shook his head. "If she'd done something to the car, the cops would have found it and she'd have been arrested."

"No one suspected her at the time, everyone just thought it was an accident because Quinn had been drinking. By the time Phil Simonson—"

"Who's he?"

"Quinn's father. By the time he asked the sheriff to check the car, someone had stripped it for parts."

"So you have nothing."

She took another drink of her beer, tore at the label some more, finally looking at him again just as coy as before, only this time it was information she was teasing him with. "She knew Josh Whitaker, the guy they found in the lake."

He stared at her. Maybe this was the solid connection he needed. "What makes you think that?" he asked, trying to keep the excitement from his voice.

"I saw him at the gas station just before he left town and disappeared."

"He could have just stopped for gas," Augustus said.

"Gas and a *kiss?* I saw him kiss her and her push him off. I couldn't hear what they were saying, but it was obvious they were arguing. He left in a huff, but not before I saw Charlie reach under his car.''

He stared at her, wishing he didn't suspect she was lying through her teeth. "And do what? Where was Josh? Where were you?''

She rolled her eyes impatiently. "I don't know what she did. I was across the street, at the general store, and I just happened to look out the window and see them. I guess Josh had gone around the side to the bathroom. I don't know.''

Augustus held her gaze. "If what you're saying is true, why didn't you tell the cops?''

"I have my reasons." She got to her feet.

"Not good enough.''

She glared down at him. "How do you know I *didn't* tell the sheriff and he didn't believe me?''

So that's the way it was.

"You don't live here," she snapped. "You don't know what it's like. Charlie Larkin can do no wrong but I tell the truth and everyone thinks I'm lying.''

He could hear the bitterness in her voice. "Why is that?''

"See," she snapped. "You even think I'm only telling you this because I have something against Charlie.''

"Don't you?''

Some of the heat went out of her gaze. "If you're asking if I'm a member of the Charlie Larkin Fan Club, I'm not. But everything I've told you is true.''

He couldn't help but be skeptical, given that the sheriff, who must know her, hadn't believed her. "The thing is, all I have is your word. Quinn and Josh are dead." Suspicion was one thing. He needed evidence and it was obvious she didn't have any. "Why don't you tell me what you have against Charlie."

She drained her beer. "You wouldn't be here asking all these questions about Charlie and the body in the lake unless you were suspicious of her. Want to tell *me* why?"

"Not really."

"I didn't think so." She set her empty beer bottle on the desk near his chair and slipped into her coat, crossing it over her breasts as she met his gaze. "You sure information is the only thing you're interested in?"

He nodded, softening the rejection with a smile, and withdrew the bills he'd put in his hip pocket earlier. It was too much for what little information she'd provided, but he had the feeling she had more to offer.

"Where does T. J. Blue fit into all this?" he asked.

She pocketed the bills without counting them. Maybe she had more class than he'd first thought. "He was Quinn Simonson's best friend." She walked to the door, stopped and turned to look at him. "If I were you, I'd be real careful. Any man who gets too close to Charlie regrets it." She smiled. "Ask Rickie Moss, if you don't believe me. He's one of the lucky ones."

CHARLIE SAW HER MOTHER to bed, waited until her aunt turned out her light for the night and then, pulling on boots and coat, decided to take a walk. At least that's the story she told herself.

The night air was crisp and cold. It had stopped snowing although ice crystals danced in the air. The sky had turned an incredible midnight blue, almost black. White clouds moved across the moon and stars sparkling like snowflakes over her head.

She kicked up the light powdery snowfall as she took the shortcut. Getting from town to the old farmhouse where she lived required driving north, then taking the county road and circling back on a narrow private road. But she could walk a few blocks and reach town if she cut through the pines and crossed the creek, a trail she had used since she was a kid, only tonight it seemed more dark and isolated than she remembered.

As she passed Murphy's she spotted Trudi's car parked near one of the cabins, steam rising off the hood, tracks cutting through the snow to cabin number five, the only one with a light on.

Charlie kept walking, telling herself there was no cause for concern, and yet she couldn't help but wonder what Augustus T. Riley would want with Trudi beyond the obvious. Maybe that's all there was to it. Just a little female company for the night.

The outside neon was turned off, the café closed for the night, but an interior light still burned and she could see someone moving around inside. She tapped at the door and Helen came to answer.

"I thought you might be by," Helen said, holding the door open. Charlie stepped in and she locked the door behind her.

"I had a craving for your coffee," she said.

Helen laughed. "I just happen to have the dregs of a pot waiting just for you. How about a piece of pie with it?"

Charlie shook her head as she slid onto the second

stool from the end. "Selma made Dutch apple for dessert."

"Damn, that sounds good." She put two cups of coffee on the counter and took the empty stool next to her. "You can't get that woman to slow down, can you?"

Charlie shook her head. "I think if she stopped fussing over me and Mom she would wither and die."

Helen cradled her coffee cup in her hands. "I talked to Maybelle," she said, staring into the black liquid. "She said he was real unfriendly and acted suspicious."

They both knew who she was talking about. "You know how nosy Maybelle is," Charlie said. Augustus T. Riley didn't seem like a man who would take well to being questioned.

"He tried to use a credit card," Helen continued. "Had a whole lot of money in his wallet. You don't think he robbed a bank or something, do you?"

Charlie smiled to herself, knowing how this town loved to talk. It seemed to thrive on stories and never got tired of repeating favorites, embellishing when necessary. As Helen always said, "No reason to tell a story if you aren't going to make it good."

"He's probably passing through just like he said," Charlie told her now.

Helen harrumphed. "You know better than that. No one just passes through Utopia. It's not like we're on the interstate or even on the road to anywhere." She said it with a kind of local pride that Charlie understood only too well. There wasn't anyplace like Utopia, locals always said. And it was so true.

"Maybe he got lost," Charlie suggested and took a sip of coffee.

"Maybe." Helen didn't sound convinced. She filled Charlie in on everything that was said at the café. "What's wrong with his car?"

"I haven't had a chance to look at it," Charlie told her. Pretty much true.

"Well, it just seems odd. Especially now."

Yes, especially now. "He asked if I was *married?*" Charlie smiled, trying to make light of it.

Helen pulled a face. "I think he might be interested in you."

Now, *that* Charlie believed, but not in the way Helen was thinking.

"There's something else," Helen said. "Trudi hightailed it out of here before we closed."

Charlie nodded and told her that she'd seen Trudi's car parked at Murphy's.

"That girl is such a tramp," Helen said. "Although, even I have to admit, he's damn good-looking."

Yes, wasn't he though? Charlie thought about Augustus T. Riley and Trudi. Maybe she'd overestimated him. If he could be distracted by someone like Trudi, maybe he wasn't as dangerous as she'd suspected. The thought made her feel a little better.

She finished her coffee. "I better get home." She started to take her cup to the back, but Helen shooed her out.

"You just fix that ol' boy's car in the morning and get him on the road," she said. "Mark my words, he's trouble."

Trouble, yes. But fixing his car wasn't going to solve the problem. She would bet on that.

As she walked back home, a snowy darkness had settled over the town, bringing with it a modicum of peace. The heavens twinkled, bright with stars, the moon setting the fallen snow aglitter.

On the edge of town, she glanced across the highway toward Murphy's. With a sinking feeling she saw that Trudi's car was already gone. So was her moment of peace.

Chapter Six

After a sleepless night, Charlie picked up the phone and dialed the number she'd memorized from Augustus T. Riley's car rental agreement. It was time to find out exactly who Augustus T. Riley was and what he wanted.

A woman answered. It took Charlie a few seconds to realize what she'd said.

A book publisher? "I must have dialed the wrong number," Charlie managed to say. "I was calling for Augustus T. Riley."

"Yes, Mr. Riley is one of our authors. I'm his publicist. What can I do for you?"

An author? She'd expected him to be a private detective. Or maybe an insurance investigator. But an author?

"What does he write?" she asked, feeling confused and wondering if she could have been wrong about Gus.

But then the publicist said, "True-crime books."

True crime?

"I'd be happy to send you a list of his books or

an autographed bookmark,'' the woman offered. ''Just give me your address—''

Charlie hung up. She stood for a moment looking at the phone. After a few moments, she walked over to her computer in the corner of the bedroom and booted it up. Within a few minutes she was typing in Augustus T. Riley under ''author'' at one of the major online bookstores. All of the Rileys came up and she scrolled down, stopping on the first Augustus T. Riley title.

Her heart begun to pound, her fingers on the mouse shaking. As she went from title to title, blurb to blurb, she saw a clear pattern in his subject matter.

Augustus T. Riley, it seemed, liked to write about women who killed their lovers or husbands.

AUGUSTUS WOKE to the sun and snow. He opened his eyes amazed at how bright the day was outside the cowboy curtains. When he'd pushed them aside, he'd been blinded by the sun glistening on the new-fallen snow—and awed by the beauty. He'd never seen anything like it. Not the depth of the blue overhead or the extremes of contrast between sky and snow and sun.

But as beautiful as it was, it was also damn cold when he'd opened the door and he was ill prepared for it. His first stop was Emmett's general store, then he walked down to Larkin & Sons Gas and Garage to the pay phone, hoping to beat Charlie there.

He'd done a lot of thinking about Charlie last night after talking to Trudi. In fact he'd been able to think of nothing else. But he still had no evidence against her. Just rumor and innuendo. Nothing concrete. But today was a new day and at least now he had some-place to start, thanks to Trudi.

He dialed Miles Baker's number. With the time difference, it was two hours later in Texas but he knew Miles would be waiting for his call no matter what the time. He and Miles had been fraternity brothers at college and as different as day and night, but had formed a friendship that had survived their major differences.

Augustus had grown up in Laguna Beach, Califor-nia, spending most of his life on a skateboard or a surfboard. Miles Baker had come from serious Texas oil wealth and a family deep in politics. From birth, Miles had been groomed to be the governor of Texas. His father was a state senator and there was talk of a chance at the presidency.

"Charlie Larkin is a woman," Augustus said with little preamble. "About twenty-six, cute as hell and adored by most everyone in this Podunk town. She's a car mechanic, owns a little garage she took over from her father."

"A woman?" Miles said. "That makes more sense, doesn't it, since we know Josh had gotten in-volved with some woman he met through the help line. So there could have been a romantic relationship. And we know that Larkin was possibly either a help-line volunteer or a client. You still think she's re-sponsible for his death?"

"It's too early to say," Augustus hedged. "Any-thing new at your end?" Miles had always had a way of getting information either through connections—or with cash.

"A gold locket was found in Josh's pocket," Miles

said. "The locket had a photo inside. But it had de-
teriorated. There was something engraved on the back
though. The words 'Love, Quinn.' Who's this
Quinn?"

"Maybe her first victim," Augustus told him and
repeated what he'd gotten from Trudi. "I'll talk to
the Simonson family today."

"If she's the killer, you'll see that she's caught,"
Miles said with confidence.

"I'll get her." He thought of the woman he'd met
last night inside the garage, how she'd let him go on
thinking she wasn't Charlie Larkin, how she'd kept
his car when it was obvious she could have fixed it.
Oh, yeah, he'd get her.

He hung up the phone. Josh had called this same
pay phone before his death. Augustus closed his eyes,
the pain blinding. He'd always been able to lose himself in the investigations, distance himself from the
crimes as just the person who was writing it all down,
trying to get to the truth.

Right now, he was fighting like hell to find some
distance, needing it desperately. He was too close, too
involved.

He opened his eyes, took a deep breath, the cold
air filling his lungs as he tried to settle down. All he
had to do was get to the truth and he'd done that
dozens of other times. He was good at this. And he
already had Charlie Larkin in his sights and was closing in.

WHEN CHARLIE DROVE UP to the garage she spotted
Augustus standing out front, obviously waiting for
her. She thought about confronting him, demanding

to know why he'd been asking questions about her and what he hoped to accomplish in Utopia.

But she feared the answer. Was it possible he'd come here because he thought she'd murdered Josh Whitaker? Surely he couldn't be thinking of writing a book about her. She told herself she was just being paranoid. Augustus T. Riley knew nothing that could harm her. At least not yet.

And there was always the chance that once she fixed his car he would be gone.

She parked alongside the garage and walked around to the front where he stood. He radiated an energy that wasn't all impatience. Her heart kicked up a beat, her traitorous body responding instinctively, nipples hardening as if the temperature had suddenly dropped.

"Morning, Gus," she said, trying to sound casual as she walked past him to the front door of the gas station.

He seemed to bristle at either her calling him Gus or just the sight of her. He'd obviously been pacing. She could see his tracks in the snow by the front door. And by the pay phone. He'd made one long call or several short ones—from the number of steps he'd taken the length of the cord.

"Good *morning*," he said and glanced pointedly at his watch, giving her a glimpse of his wrist, the skin tanned.

The watch was expensive. Like the shirt. The coat new, something he'd obviously just purchased that morning at Emmett's store. It looked odd on him, maybe because she couldn't imagine him wearing it anywhere but in Utopia.

That thought was like a weight crushing her chest, making it hard to breathe. He planned to stay around a while.

"I hope I didn't keep you waiting." She caught his reflection in the glass as she unlocked the door and felt strangely pleased that he'd recognized her comment for what it was: sarcasm. So many men didn't get sarcasm.

"It's off-season," she said, just in case he hadn't figured that out yet.

"What if someone needs gas to get out of here?" he asked, sounding irritable as he followed her inside.

She went around behind the counter and busied herself, her back to him. "The pumps are always open. Customers just leave their money in that can on top of the second pump. We work with an honor system."

"You have to be kidding."

She turned, his shocked expression making her smile. "Welcome to Utopia." She'd meant it as a joke.

"Thanks." His eyes narrowed, his gaze suddenly much more personal. "You could have told me last night you were Charlie Larkin," he said, voice low and soft as a caress.

"I thought it was obvious." She pointed to the stitching on her clean baggy overalls.

"In some places Charlie is considered a man's name."

"Is it? I'll bet in those places being a mechanic is still male territory as well."

He didn't respond.

She realized that something had changed since last

night. The way he was looking at her. It was subtle at first, then more direct. He was looking at her as if trying to see inside her.

She felt her skin burn under all the clothing she'd put on this morning. She'd purposely dressed in long underwear, an old flannel shirt of her dad's, her baggiest overalls, boots and an old canvas jacket. And yet she felt naked under his gaze.

"About your car—"

"Yes, my car." A muscle jerked in his jaw. "You think you can fix it?"

He definitely understood sarcasm. Obviously he knew how easy it would be to get the engine running properly again. He could probably fix it himself in a matter of minutes. After all, he'd been the one to foul it up to start with. So, he either thought she wasn't much of a mechanic. Or that she was playing him for a fool.

Who was the fool here? she wondered as she stepped past him toward the first bay, feeling the need for more distance between them. "I took a look at your car last night and I've got some bad news." She could hear him behind her, his steps echoing solidly on the concrete floor. She could almost feel his disbelief. She smiled to herself in spite of the voice in her head that was screaming: What in the devil are you doing?

"It looks like I'm going to have to order in some parts." She stopped and turned to look at him, daring him to show his hand.

He looked flabbergasted. "You aren't serious?"

She raised an eyebrow. "You know how bad it was running when you brought it in. What did you think?

That it would take just a few minor adjustments to get it going again?'' Which was exactly what it *would* take.

She waited, giving him a chance to confess and offer up a good excuse for why he'd screwed up his carburetor, why he'd pretended to need a mechanic, why he'd been looking for Charlie Larkin in the first place.

She could see the battle going on in his eyes. Deep dark blue eyes like the lightless bottom of the ocean. Or Freeze Out Lake. It was clear he wanted to call her bluff and wanted to badly.

''Parts, huh?'' His jaw was rigid as he turned away from her. ''And what exactly is wrong with the car?''

''If you want, I can write up an estimate later but I really don't have time to go into it now.'' She watched him clench his hands into fists, his broad, muscular back to her, suddenly making her take notice of his size. Six-two or -three. Strong-looking, as if he lifted weights regularly.

Her gaze dropped to the jeans he wore and the muscled legs she could make out through the denim. A flicker of heat a lot like desire found flame inside her. She quickly doused the fire as she noticed the new winter boots. Why would a man from L.A. who was just passing through town buy snowpacks?

He turned so swiftly, startling her how fast he could move. She wouldn't stand a chance against him physically, she thought. Not without the benefit of surprise. And a weapon.

But she knew that wasn't what she had to fear from Augustus T. Riley. It was the way he made her feel. Vulnerable, the way an animal can sense weakness in his prey. It was as if Gus could see beneath the baggy clothing to that unfulfilled ache deep within her like an Achilles' heel he could use to destroy her. He couldn't have been more dangerous.

He stepped toward her, his gaze so intense she almost recoiled. The air seemed to crackle with tension. In the time and space it took for him to close the space between them, the tension changed to purely chemical. Helen was right; the man was incredibly good-looking. But that wasn't the half of it.

"How long do you think it will take?" he asked, his voice silky, the air alive with more electricity than her heavy-duty battery charger in the corner.

She shrugged, trying hard to hide the effect he was having on her. Her face seemed flushed although it was still cold in the garage and her eyes felt too bright, as if she'd had too much coffee.

Her voice sounded strange to her as she said, "I'll see if I can get parts from Missoula sent overnight, then do a complete inventory of what I'll need and check to see if the parts store there has them in stock."

"It's not like the car is some odd import."

"No," she agreed. "You might want to call your rental car agency. Maybe they can bring you another car and get you on your way. Or I can do it for you. We'll need their okay before I can work on the car anyway."

He didn't even blink. "I've already called. I'm picking up the expense for the repairs and they're going to reimburse me later. But there's no hurry."

She didn't think so. "I'll give you a call at Murphy's when I have the estimate written up." He hadn't taken the bait. She started toward the office again, wishing now that she'd just adjusted his carburetor. But she knew that wouldn't have gotten rid of him. At least this way he didn't have a car. The closest car rental was thirty miles away. He'd have to call—have a car delivered and that would take time. How much trouble could he get into on foot?

He grabbed her arm, the heat of his fingers seeming to cut right through all the fabrics to her naked skin.

She froze in midstep, her breath catching in her throat. She didn't dare look at him. Didn't dare move.

"I'm sorry if you and I got off on the wrong foot," he said quietly. His voice sounded strained. He let go of her as if suddenly feeling the charged air. Or maybe just recognizing it for what it was. "I could buy you a cup of coffee or a beer or something since I'm going to be around for a while."

"That's not necessary," she said and continued to the office and around behind the counter. She picked up the phone and began to dial. "The sooner I see what it will take to get parts shipped…"

He stood for a moment, silhouetted against the window and the blinding sunny snowy day beyond it. She couldn't see his expression, but she didn't need to. He was studying her again, looking for something. She could only guess what, given his occupation.

Her pulse throbbed in her temple, her body aquiver as if the room had been electrified. He might have come here to see her put behind bars, but if she let down her defenses, if she let him get too close, he could destroy her like no other man was capable of and she knew it.

Her hand trembled as she hit the last number and waited for the line to ring.

She didn't even know what number she'd dialed until she heard Jenny's voice. It was a number she thought she'd forgotten, it had been so long since she'd called it.

"Hello," she said much more cheerfully than she felt.

Gus gave her a nod, his large hand pushing the door open, the cold rushing in, and finally the door closed behind him. She slumped against the counter, weak with relief.

"Charlie?" Jenny Simonson sounded surprised. Almost suspicious.

She let out a sigh, fighting tears. "I don't know why I called you. Yes, I do. I've missed you. Could we get together?"

A slight hesitation on Jenny's end. Maybe still surprised. "Sure."

"Great." She felt relieved, glad she'd called, guilty that she hadn't tried to keep their friendship even after Jenny had married Forest Simonson. "How about today at the Pinecone. Say one?"

"Okay." Jenny didn't sound thrilled about the prospect.

She hung up, her hands shaking. Why had she called Jenny? Because they'd once been best friends? Or because she was looking for some sort of absolution? Maybe she just needed her friend back.

AUGUSTUS COULDN'T BELIEVE it as he started hiking down the middle of the icy highway. He couldn't believe it. Not the fact that when he'd touched her it had been like grabbing a live wire. Or the fact that she'd called his bluff. Why had he touched her? That shock of heat and electricity through all those layers of her clothing should have jolted him to his senses. Instead, he felt dazed and aroused. He hadn't felt anything like that since… He stumbled. Since Natalie.

He shook off the thought, telling himself Charlie and Natalie were nothing alike. Unless, of course, Charlie tried to kill him.

He swore, furious with his traitorous body. Hadn't he learned his lesson with Natalie? Obviously not.

And to add insult to injury, Charlie had called his damn bluff! The woman had called his bluff. She knew the engine didn't need parts. She also knew that he must have tampered with it—and had known since last night. So why had she kept the car overnight? So she could search it? Had she been onto him from the start?

But there hadn't been anything to find. Except for the rental agreement. He'd forgotten about that. Fortunately when he'd gone back last night to leave the newspaper clipping, he'd found the rental agreement right where he'd left it. But that didn't mean she hadn't seen it and didn't now know who he was—and suspected why he'd come here.

Not that he was so famous she'd recognize the name—unless she read true-crime stories. But it would be easy to find out who he was—if she wanted to or needed to.

If she knew who he was and had figured out why he'd come to Utopia, then why lie about his car needing parts?

Why keep him in town? Especially if she knew and was guilty of murder?

Maybe she ripped off every out-of-towner whose car broke down. Except if what he'd heard about her charitable acts was true...

He stopped walking, oblivious to the fact that he was standing in the middle of the icy highway, as a thought hit him. She'd kept his car to keep him on foot! Maybe she believed it would discourage him. He smiled at the thought. She'd find out that he wouldn't be discouraged that easily.

He started walking again, finding himself shaking his head in admiration. Charlie Larkin was something! He let out a frosty breath and tried to calm down. The woman had a way of setting him on edge whenever he was around her. He blamed it on being that close to a killer. But he'd been close to a lot of killers and couldn't remember any of them making him feel so...jittery when he was around any one of them. Except for Natalie.

He was reminded again of that moment in the garage when he'd touched Charlie. He frowned as he recalled the sense of heat the woman had about her, a...sexual temperature that would send mercury rocketing. Was that how she lured men into her trap? A nice guy like Josh Whitaker must have been child's play for her. It made her even more intriguing—and dangerous. He wanted to nail this woman if it was the last thing he ever did.

He heard the sound of a vehicle coming up behind him and moved over to the edge of the highway as the car slowed, then stopped. He turned, already knowing who it was.

"Need a ride, Gus?" Emmett Graham asked as he rolled down the passenger-side window. What a coincidence that Emmett had come along at just the right moment *again*.

Augustus glanced back at Larkin & Sons Gas and Garage, thought he glimpsed Charlie's small form just beyond the sun-glazed glass of the office window, thought he felt her gaze on him.

It seemed the woman wanted him on foot—and under the watchful eye of Emmett Graham. He just didn't know why she was trying to keep him in town. It was almost as if she was daring him to catch her.

"As a matter of fact, I could use a ride," he said, climbing into Emmett's car, no longer sure who was the hunter—and who was the prey.

Chapter Seven

Augustus found Rickie Moss working at the local sawmill just north of town. Emmett had been more than happy to drive him, just as Augustus had suspected he would be. And Augustus liked the idea that Charlie would know what he'd been doing. She'd know he was after her. Let her run scared. For a while.

Huge piles of tree-length logs were stacked like straws in piles around a small shack and lean-to. Augustus walked toward the buzz of a saw under the lean-to. Snow melted, dripping from the roof into several large puddles around the edifice. The air smelled of fresh-cut wood.

Two men were running long boards through the blade, cutting the wood into two-by-fours. Another two were stacking them onto the back of a flatbed.

"Rickie Moss?" Augustus yelled over the ripping whine of the blade.

One of the men on the saw motioned to a stacker to take his place. The man jumped down from the raised floor of the lean-to and walked toward him.

Rickie Moss had once been a good-looking man,

the kind of man Charlie Larkin might have been attracted to. But now a hideous scar carved across one cheek from the corner of his left eye to below his chin ravaged his face.

"I'm Rickie," the man said sourly. "What do you want?"

"I want to talk to you about Charlie Larkin," Augustus said.

Rickie Moss jerked back as if he'd been smacked. His eyes narrowed. "What about Charlie?"

"Any chance we could get away from that saw?" he asked as the blade ripped through another long board. "I'll make it worth your while." He flashed the sawmill worker a fifty.

Rickie glanced to the crew for a moment, then nodded and headed for the small shack. He shoved open the door and entered. Augustus followed.

There was just enough room inside for a man to turn around but not much more. Papers were strewn across a desk made from a broken sheet of plywood. A stool, the black vinyl cushion cracked, stuffing leaking out, was pulled up to the high desk, which also held a coffeemaker and a miniature microwave. The place smelled of stale coffee and nuked cabbage. But it was quieter.

"Yeah?" Rickie said impatiently.

"I understand you used to be Charlie's boyfriend," he said, leaping right in.

Rickie just stared at him, waiting.

"Is she the reason you have that scar?"

The question got a response out of him.

"What the hell is this about?" Rickie demanded.

''Information. I'm investigating that drowning up at Freeze Out Lake.''

Ricky didn't seem surprised to hear this. Augustus was pretty sure that was the kind of story Trudi would have told anyone who would listen to her.

Augustus laid the fifty on top of the papers on the desk. ''Why do bad things happen to men who're interested in Charlie Larkin?''

Rickie looked from him to the fifty and back up. ''I don't know.''

''What happened to you?'' He dropped another fifty on top of the first.

Rickie shook his head. ''Didn't Trudi tell you?''

''No. She just told me to talk to you.'' Augustus figured Trudi had broken the ice for him. Rickie didn't seem like the type who would have given him the time of day otherwise.

''I only went out with Charlie once. It was years ago. It wasn't even much of a date. I bought her a burger at the Pinecone, then we went for a ride.'' He met Augustus's gaze. ''Up to Freeze Out Lake.''

Augustus tried not to show his surprise.

''We drank a couple of beers, necked a little.'' He shrugged. ''I got out of the car to take a leak and something attacked me.''

''Something or *someone?*''

Rickie shook his head. ''I was hit from behind and I woke up with this.'' He ran a finger down the length of the scar.

''Where was Charlie during all this?''

Rickie picked up a pencil from the desk and turned it in his fingers. ''In the car. She said she got worried and came looking for me. She's the one who found me and got me to the doctor.''

"You believe her?"

He dropped the pencil and picked up the fifties, taking his time to fold them and put them into his flannel shirt pocket. "What do you think?"

"I think you're scared of her."

Rickie smiled. "A little thing like her? Now what kind of man would that make me?"

"Possibly a smart one?"

"I have to get back to work," Rickie said but didn't move.

"Are you trying to tell me that every man she's dated met with an accident?" Augustus asked. "Like maybe there's a curse on her?" He realized he was only half joking.

Rickie shrugged and looked a little embarrassed. "I just know what happened to T.J. when he tried to date her. And then to me. Maybe she dated at college and didn't have any problems."

"T. J. Blue?" Augustus asked.

Rickie nodded.

"I thought he was Quinn's best friend?"

"Quinn was dead and Charlie—well, Charlie is a fine-looking woman," Rickie said.

She was a lot more than that, Augustus thought. "What happened to T.J.?"

"One date and his trailer burned down. He barely got out with his life." Rickie shook his head. "All I know is that no one around here is fool enough to get within twenty feet of her." He raised an eyebrow.

Augustus shook his head. "Don't look at me."

Rickie laughed. "Smart man."

T. J. BLUE WORKED at a small wild-game processing plant north of town during hunting season, according to Emmett, who offered to drive Gus.

Augustus realized he was even starting to think of himself as "Gus" now, and he had Charlie to blame for that.

T.J. was standing on the frosty concrete floor beside a carcass-covered metal table, feeding strips of moose meat into a commercial-size meat grinder when Gus walked in. The freezer-cold air smelled of suet and sweat, the sound of the grinder echoing in the refrigerator-like room.

Blond with blue eyes, T. J. Blue wore a white butcher's smock splattered with blood and bits of dried red meat over winter clothes, his massive hands clad in gloves that had probably once been white.

Next to him, a dark-haired young woman sliced pieces of meat from a carcass with a knife. She glanced at Gus, her gaze hanging on him just long enough to make him pretty sure she knew who he was. T.J. gave him only a passing glance and kept dropping meat and chunks of suet into the grinder.

"Got a minute?" Gus yelled over the growl of the grinder.

T. J. Blue shot him a look that said Gus would be damn lucky to get a second out of him.

To Gus's surprise, the woman reached over and shut off the grinder. "Why don't you take a break," she said to T.J.

He gave her a dirty look. "If I need a break, I'll let you know, Earlene," he growled, but jerked off his gloves, threw them down, then turned and headed toward a door at the back.

"Break room's back there," Earlene said and flopped the carcass over and picked up her knife.

Gus watched her trim meat from the carcass with obvious skill, before he followed T.J. through the door into the break room at the back of the plant. The room was warmer than the meat shop, but not by much.

T.J. poured himself a cup of coffee, then turned to look at Gus with obvious irritation. "I know who you are, but I don't have anything to say to you."

So much of getting people to talk to you was making them think you had the right to know what they had to tell you. "Then you don't think Charlie murdered Quinn," Gus said.

T.J. jerked back in surprise. "I don't think about Charlie Larkin at all."

Gus didn't believe that for a minute. "You don't seem to like her."

"What makes you think that?"

"The way you left the café last night. Tell me about Charlie Larkin," Gus pushed. "Tell me why you and every other male in this town with any sense is afraid of her."

A muscle jumped in T. J. Blue's jaw. "I have nothing to say to you." He threw the coffee into the sink, slammed down the cup and left Gus standing alone in the break room wondering for the first time about Charlie's motive.

All of this seemed to have started with Quinn Simonson. Was it possible she felt guilty about Quinn's death and hurt men who wanted to date her as some sort of warped penance? Or was it payback? Trudi said the night Quinn died Charlie had just found out that Earlene was carrying Quinn's baby. That would tick off most any woman. Gus wondered if Charlie had been mad enough to kill? And if she had, had she just gone on hurting men, killing the less fortunate ones?

"Get what you needed, Gus?" Emmett asked as he drove back to town.

Augustus watched the dense dark pines flicker past. "How long have you lived here?"

"All my life," the old man said proudly. "Born and raised. Can't find a nicer little town to settle down in. Graham's General Store has been in that very spot for almost a hundred years. My father opened it back when this part of the country was nothing but wilderness."

As far as Gus was concerned it was still wilderness.

"At one time in its history, this town was booming," Emmett was saying. "But the mines closed, the logging industry went to pot, people moved on. Times change."

Gus couldn't imagine a lifetime here.

"It's busier in the summers," Emmett continued. "Fly fishermen, tourists up here for Glacier and Yellowstone Parks, people looking for back roads, looking for another, more simple time and place. That's Utopia."

Emmett stopped in front of Murphy's. "Is there anywhere else I can give you a ride to, Gus?"

"No thanks," he said as he got out of the car. "Don't you have a store to run?"

Emmett laughed. "This time of year it's a little slow, so my wife would just as soon I wasn't underfoot." He winked at Gus. "Truth is, she's really the

boss. Just let me know if I can be of any help, Gus,''
he said, then glanced at his watch. ''The lunch special
at the café is tuna melt. You might want to beat the
rush.''

''Thanks.'' He smiled to himself as he watched
Emmett drive off. Beat the rush. But his smile faded
as he saw Emmett pull into one of the gas pumps at
Larkin's. Charlie came out. Emmett didn't need gas.
Gus had seen the gauge. It was on Full.

After a moment of obvious discussion, he saw
Charlie glance down the highway in his direction. He
waved and walked toward the café. He'd pass on the
tuna melt, but he could use a cheeseburger and fries.
At the very least, maybe Trudi would be working.
He'd just bet she'd know where he could find Phil
Simonson this time of the day.

THE PINECONE CAFÉ was nearly empty when Charlie
came in a few minutes after one. Jenny Simonson was
sitting alone in the back booth. She looked nervous
as she glanced out at the street and Charlie wondered
if she'd told Forest they were having lunch together.

''Hi,'' Charlie said, more glad to see her than Jenny
could ever know. She slid into the booth across from
her once–best friend, wanting desperately to feel that
old connection, needing it now more than ever.

''Hi.'' Jenny's smile didn't quite reach her eyes.

''You look great!'' It wasn't quite true. Jenny had
changed over the years. She was thinner, her face
drawn, making her dark eyes seem too large. Her once
long, beautiful dark hair had been cut to her chin. It
hung straight, all the shine gone from it—just like her

eyes. Either marriage to Forest Simonson had aged her or motherhood had.

"So do you," Jenny said, a clear lie. Charlie had been having trouble sleeping since Josh's body was found. Actually long before that.

"So how is Skye?" Charlie asked. "Shoot, she must be how old by now?"

Jenny flushed and Charlie could have kicked herself for bringing up Skye's age although everyone in the county knew Jenny and Forest had had to get married right out of high school. Right after Quinn's death. "She's almost seven."

In the silence that hung between them, Trudi bopped up to give them menus. Helen was busy in the back washing the lunch dishes, but had waved as Charlie came in.

"I've missed you," Charlie said, hoping to find even a little of what she and Jenny had once shared in this almost stranger sitting across from her now.

Jenny nodded, looking uncomfortable, and glanced again to the street. "I've missed you, too."

"Forest doesn't know you're here, does he?" Charlie said, feeling sick at the realization.

Jenny's gaze jerked back to her in surprise, the first honest reaction Charlie had gotten out of her.

"It's okay. I understand." Jenny had made her choice when she'd married Forest, married into a family that had made hating Charlie Larkin into a religion because of Quinn's death. Fortunately, few people listened to the Simonsons' rantings and ravings or Charlie would be behind bars by now.

Jenny shook her head, tears in her eyes. "He's my husband."

Charlie nodded and reached across the table to squeeze her hand, realizing the courage it had taken Jenny to come here. "I know. This must be very hard for you. I shouldn't have asked you to do this."

"What? Have lunch?" Jenny said, pulling back her hand as she busied herself looking for a tissue in her purse. She sounded angry and upset. "I should be able to have lunch with anyone I want to. It's just that Forest—" She looked up, fresh tears flooded her eyes.

Charlie nodded. "Lunch was a bad idea. I'm sorry."

Jenny seemed to be fighting tears and losing the battle. She stumbled to her feet. "I'm the one who's sorry," she said and rushed out of the café.

Charlie sat staring down at the menus, shaking inside, wanting to go after Jenny, wanting to confront Forest and the rest of the Simonsons, wanting to just sit in the booth and cry.

"She coming back?" Trudi asked, standing over Charlie, her obvious curiosity about killing her.

"She just remembered that she left her oven on," Charlie said dispassionately.

Trudi smirked. "That's too bad."

Charlie reined in her emotions and looked at Trudi, wondering what had happened last night in Augustus T. Riley's cabin at Murphy's. It was better than thinking about Jenny and everything that had been lost between them.

"So what are you going to have?" Trudi asked.

"Get us both a bowl of the soup," Helen said, slipping into the booth across from Charlie. Charlie started to tell her the last thing she wanted right now was food, but Helen cut her off. "You have to eat and you know my seafood bisque is to die for."

Poor choice of words. But Charlie appreciated the sentiment. She smiled at Helen, grateful for friends like her.

"Don't let those Simonsons get to you," Helen said. "They're all a spineless bunch. If Jenny hadn't gotten pregnant, she'd never have married the likes of Forest Simonson and everyone in town knows it."

Trudi slid a couple of bowls of seafood bisque onto the table and a handful of crackers in plastic sleeves. "You want anything else?"

Helen waved her away. "I swear, sometimes I wonder why I keep that girl on."

They both knew why. Finding anyone who'd stay in Utopia and work was getting harder and harder as the older residents moved to Arizona and the younger ones moved to someplace that had a real video store.

"Are you okay?" Helen asked after she'd insisted Charlie eat some of her soup.

Charlie nodded, although she was far from okay. The soup could have been water for her ability to taste it.

"He was in for lunch," Helen said after a moment as if wanting to get all the bad news over with. "He got directions to Phil Simonson's place from Trudi."

Charlie nodded again, wondering if anything would surprise her at this point. Outside, the snow had melted off the black pavement. The gutters ran full with the runoff. Only a few patches of snow remained in the shade of the buildings and in the trees as the day warmed back to normal temperatures.

"What does he want?" Helen asked quietly.

Charlie shook her head, afraid she knew exactly what he wanted.

"I can give you the name of a private investigator I hired once out of Missoula. He got the goods on Frank." Frank was one of Helen's husbands. Charlie couldn't remember which.

But the last thing she wanted to do was involve a private investigator. "Let me do some digging on my own first."

Helen wrote down the investigator's name on her napkin. "Don't wait too long."

She took the napkin, her gaze locking with Helen's for a long moment. How much did Helen suspect? "Thanks."

Chapter Eight

Phil Simonson lived a short walk back in the pines in an A-frame cabin. He'd been a logger, Trudi had said, until he'd gotten hurt four years ago. Now he lived on disability and what he could make as a chain-saw artist.

Gus followed the buzz of a saw around to the back of the house.

Standing in a pile of wood chips and sawdust was a short, stocky man, bucking a chain saw. Before him, a large piece of log was being chewed into the shape of a bear.

"Hello!" Gus called out, but the saw was too loud for Phil to have heard. He moved closer and waited.

Phil finally glanced up, not looking surprised to see him. He shut off the saw and dropped it to the sawdust. It took a moment for the silence to settle in as Phil dusted off his hands on his dirty wool pants.

"I was just getting ready to take a break," the ex-logger said, turning to head for the house. He walked with an exaggerated limp as if his right leg was a good six inches shorter than his left. "Coffee's on. Wanna cup?"

"Sure." Gus followed him inside the house to the kitchen where Phil motioned for him to take a seat at the breakfast bar. The house was cluttered like a man's who lived alone. Trudi hadn't mentioned Phil's marital status, but Gus would bet divorced. There were enough cute things on the walls to suggest a woman's hand. And enough dust on them to suggest she'd been gone for some time.

Phil set a mug of steaming black coffee before him. "I've got some milk. No cream." He shoved a sugar bowl in his direction.

"Black is fine," Gus said. He didn't plan to drink much of it anyway. It looked like liquid sludge.

"So what do you want to know?" Phil asked, leaning into the counter across from him. "I heard you were investigating the latest murder."

Good ol' Trudi. But Gus knew the easy ones wanted to talk, to get their side out, to point fingers. They didn't care who they told. Or what that person wanted with the information. Getting them to talk wasn't the problem. Getting them to tell the truth was. "Tell me about Charlie Larkin."

Phil took a sip of his coffee. "She killed my boy."

Without any coaxing, Phil told him about how his son had fallen for Charlie Larkin at a young tender age. "There'd never been another girl for Quinn," Phil said. "All he talked about was how smart she was, how pretty, how someday he was going to marry her. But Charlie had other ideas."

Charlie and Quinn had graduated from high school a few days before the accident. Schools were in Libby, thirty miles away. Utopia students had to be bused there each school day. Gus couldn't imagine going so far to school and on such treacherous roads.

"Charlie didn't want to get married," Phil was saying. "It seemed she wanted to go to college, and since Quinn was planning to stay here to log with me, he was history." Phil sounded as bitter as his coffee tasted.

"I heard Quinn had gotten another girl pregnant," Gus said, trying to get a little truth out of the man.

Phil made a face. "Earlene. I'm not saying my boy was perfect. He made a mistake with Earlene, but that doesn't mean he had to lose Charlie. Quinn was trying his damnedest to keep from losing her the night he died. That's what makes it all so unfair."

"How did they end up at the lake then?" Gus asked, not wanting to talk about fair.

Phil shrugged. "A bunch of Quinn's friends were at a party up there. I knew he wanted to go. I heard him and Charlie arguing on the phone. I know Charlie didn't want to go but maybe he talked her into it."

Or maybe Quinn had just driven up there anyway, Gus thought, once he had her in the car.

"They got in a huge fight at the party," Phil said as he went over to a shelf in the dining room and took down a photograph framed in silver plastic. "Everyone saw it. Quinn had had a few beers with his friends. He left, driving fast. The sheriff thought that's what caused the accident. It wasn't until later that anyone remembered Charlie had worked on Quinn's car the day before and she'd been over by the car just before he left." Phil nodded as if that pretty much said it all and handed Gus the framed photo.

It was of a young man, blond and blue-eyed, handsome as Adonis. Quinn Simonson had looked nothing like his father and Gus wondered if he'd taken after his mother.

"But no one saw Charlie do anything to the car that night?" he asked.

"She's a damn mechanic," Phil snapped. "How long would it take her to cut a brake line or do something to the steering?"

He didn't know. He set the photo on the breakfast bar. Unlike everything else that was on the shelf, the frame was dustless as if it had been taken down so many times it had been wiped clean.

"What do you think her intent was?" Gus asked. "I mean, why kill him? What did she have to gain?"

Phil studied the coffee scum at the bottom of his cup. "Who knows what she was thinking?—she's a woman."

She couldn't have known the crash would kill him—or even if he would crash, Gus thought. It seemed a damn inefficient way to try to murder someone. But maybe Phil was right. Maybe, since Quinn was allegedly her first victim, maybe her actions had been just hotheaded.

Except for one thing. Charlie Larkin didn't strike him as a hothead.

"She killed him," Phil said and took his coffee cup over to the sink.

Gus heard a pickup in need of a muffler come roaring up outside the A-frame.

Phil didn't seem to hear it. A few moments later a young man who resembled Phil came through the door. He had the same stocky build, the same intense dark eyes, the same unruly dark hair and beard. He wasn't bad-looking, he just did nothing to improve his appearance.

"This that Gus guy who's asking around about Charlie?" the young man demanded, never taking those eyes off Gus.

"My son, Forest," Phil said as if Forest's manners were of no concern to him.

Gus held out his hand. "Augustus T. Riley."

Forest smirked. "That's a pretty highfalutin name. What is it you do that calls for a name like that?"

"It's just the name my parents gave me," Gus said, getting his back up. "I'm a crime writer," he said, deciding it was time to lay his cards on the table.

Phil let out a curse. "A writer? I thought he was a private detective." The older man mumbled to himself. "What's a writer going to do about my son's murder?"

Gus noticed the young woman and child who'd come in behind Forest Simonson. The dark-haired woman stood by the door, her hands on the little girl's shoulders, a wary look in the woman's eyes. "Hello," he said, looking past Forest to her.

The woman gave him a nod and said nothing. Her hair was chin length and straight, framing a pale face and large dark eyes. She looked to be about Charlie Larkin's age.

Phil glanced toward the door, his gaze immediately dismissing the two as he said, "My daughter-in-law, Jenny, and Skye," adding almost like an afterthought, "my granddaughter." The way he said "granddaughter" it was clear he would have much preferred a grandson.

Forest poured himself a mug of coffee, then opened the refrigerator door to scrounge around inside. He came out with a piece of cold grocery-store pizza. "So you going to write about Charlie and what she done, Gus?" he asked, taking a huge bite of the pizza.

"Maybe. If she's done anything."

Forest made an ugly face. "She killed my brother." He turned to his father. "Didn't you tell him that?"

"I told him," Phil said.

"But you have no proof of that," Gus pointed out.

Jenny hadn't moved from the doorway. Nor had Skye. And Phil hadn't offered either of them anything to eat or drink or even a chair.

Gus could see why the sheriff hadn't taken the male Simonsons' accusations seriously. They were way too bitter over Quinn's death, bloodthirsty for vengeance, and right or wrong, had found someone to blame—Charlie.

"Charlie wouldn't—" Jenny's words were cut short by her husband's.

"I don't want to hear a word out of you," Forest bellowed, jabbing a warning finger at his wife. "I won't have you defending that woman in my house."

It was the man's father's house, but that didn't seem to make any difference.

"Did any of you know Josh Whitaker?" Gus asked into the tense silence.

Phil and Forest shared a puzzled look.

"The man whose body was recently pulled out of Freeze Out Lake," Gus prompted. "He was a doctor in the emergency room at the hospital in Missoula."

"Oh, yeah, I heard about that," Forest said. "Why would we know him?" He sounded suspicious.

Gus shrugged. "Just wondering since the sheriff's department found a gold locket on Josh that according to my sources might have belonged to Charlie Larkin." He saw Phil's eyes widen. The older man let out a curse.

"That's the locket Quinn gave Charlie," Phil said. "It was engraved on the back: Love, Quinn. What was this man doing with it?"

Gus shook his head. "I thought you might know."

"Where do you *think* he got it?" Forest demanded. "From Charlie Larkin, that's where."

"Why would Charlie give him a locket that Quinn had given her?" Gus asked.

"How the hell do I know?" Forest snapped. "Why don't you ask the lying bitch? Maybe she killed this Josh guy, too. Hell, I wouldn't put it past her." He glanced toward Jenny.

She was staring at the floor, her husband watching her as if he expected her to say something. Gus could feel the tension between them tight as piano wire. He wondered if Charlie was the only thing causing it.

Jenny ran a hand over her daughter's long blond hair, and when she finally looked at her husband there was a chilling hatred in her gaze.

Gus pushed his almost-full mug of coffee away and got up. "Thanks for the coffee," he said to Phil. He nodded to Forest and started toward the door.

"Wait a minute," Forest said. "What are you going to do about my brother's murder?"

Gus stopped and turned to look at the man. He didn't like him, couldn't imagine why Jenny had married him, but suspected it had something to do with the child. "It isn't my job to do anything about your brother's death. I'm not even sure he was murdered."

Phil jumped in. "Well, this other guy, Josh…"

"Whitaker," Gus provided.

"He was murdered," Phil noted.

"Yes," Gus agreed. "But there's no proof Charlie Larkin did it."

Forest slammed down his coffee cup, spilling coffee all over the kitchen counter. "You sound just like that damn sheriff of ours. Everyone knows Charlie's a killer, but no one has the guts to do anything about it." He glared at Gus.

"Thanks again for the coffee," Gus said to Phil. "It was nice meeting you," he said to Jenny and Skye on his way out. To his surprise, Jenny followed him out the door, closing it behind her.

"Charlie didn't kill Quinn," Jenny said in a burst of emotion. "It was just an accident. Just an awful accident."

He studied her, thinking at one time she might have been quite pretty. "How do you know that?"

"I know…Charlie."

Gus glanced toward the house. He could see Phil and Forest Simonson watching out the window. He had a bad feeling that Jenny shouldn't have come after him, that it would get her into more trouble and she was already in enough. "What about Josh Whitaker?"

"Charlie wouldn't hurt anyone. Look how Charlie's helped Earlene and her baby when the Simonsons' wouldn't even give her the time of day." Jenny shook her head, tears rushing her eyes. She stepped back, then turned and ran to the house, no doubt realizing that she shouldn't have come out here.

Gus felt cold inside as he walked back toward the main drag. All he wanted to do at the moment was put some distance between himself and the Simonsons and the bad feeling they gave him.

Chapter Nine

When Gus got back to the motel, he had a FedEx package waiting for him in the office from Miles. He could see that Maybelle Murphy was just dying to know what was inside it and hoping he'd open it in front of her. Fat chance.

"Oh," she said with obvious disappointment as he started to leave. "You also have a message from Charlie Larkin about your car."

"What about my car?" he asked, turning to look back at the woman. She was all duded out again today and smelled to high heaven.

Maybelle shrugged. "She wouldn't say. Just that you are to see her about your car." It sounded as if it just hadn't been Maybelle's day when it came to finding out anything interesting. But life was full of disappointments.

He left the office, wondering what Charlie planned to tell him about the car now. Maybe that he needed a new transmission? Or maybe a complete overhaul?

He went to his cabin and opened the FedEx envelope from Miles. As promised, Miles had used his influence to get as much information as possible on any contacts Josh might have made with other residents of Utopia—besides Charlie Larkin.

Being an emergency room doctor, Josh could have treated someone from Utopia. It was a long shot, since the hospital in Libby was closer, but Gus had asked him to try to get that information any way he could. Wealthy and in line to be the next governor of Texas, Miles had his ways.

Gus was surprised to see that Josh had been working in the emergency room on two different occasions when residents of Utopia had been brought in. The first was when Phil Simonson had his logging accident and was taken to Missoula. That meant Josh might have met the whole family, including Forest. The second was when Earlene Kurtz had taken her son, Arnie, in for an asthma attack while shopping in Missoula.

Gus took the time to type up his notes from the morning on his laptop, then decided he'd better find out what Charlie wanted. He thought about walking over to the Pinecone and calling her from there, but decided he preferred to see her face when she lied to him again, and the walk would do him good. He didn't feel any closer to catching Josh's killer than when he'd hit town.

With the sun lower in the sky, the air was colder, the fallen snow a light silken gray. He wrapped his coat around him and started walking down the highway toward Larkin & Sons Gas and Garage, thinking about what the Simonsons had told him. The bad part was he'd *wanted* to believe them about Charlie's guilt—and couldn't. So far, all he'd heard was accusations and insinuations with nothing to back them up.

He looked up, surprised at how quickly he'd made the walk and relieved to see that Charlie's van was parked along the side. He pushed open the door to the gas station.

She wasn't in the office, but then he hadn't expected her to be. The air felt cool and smelled of grease and oil as he stopped in the doorway to the garage. He could see his rental car in the second bay.

Charlie was bent over the fender of an older-model black pickup in the first bay. A slow country song played on the radio, the volume much lower than it had been the night before.

He stood there in the doorway just studying her backside wondering about her. Also wondering if he'd only imagined the electricity he thought he'd felt earlier when he'd touched her. It was clear to him that he was going to have to get a whole lot closer to her if he hoped to find out the truth—and he feared just how dangerous that could be.

Resigned, he moved toward her, surprised when he picked up the faint scent of flowers as he neared her. Was it possible Charlie was wearing perfume? The thought more than surprised him, it intrigued him, given the way she dressed. He followed the enticing fragrance as he quietly moved closer and closer until he was just inches from her.

Was this how she spun her deadly web? With something as innocuous as a sweet scent emanating from beneath layers of baggy clothing? What was she hiding under all those clothes? He could imagine a man being captivated by such a mystery. It was enough to make any man want to peel away the layers, one after another, leisurely, watchfully, until there was nothing Charlie Larkin could keep secret from him.

He leaned over her, breathing her in. It wasn't perfume. Too light. Had to be soap. She smelled fresh from a shower as if she was still damp and radiated a humid kind of succulence, her skin burning hot under all the clothes she wore.

The beguiling scents mingled around her, so at odds with the smells of the garage, reminding him Charlie Larkin was definitely feminine beneath those overalls—though it was obvious she tried damn hard to hide it.

Or maybe that was her allure—the way she hid her femininity, her sexuality...her duplicity.

He breathed her in, needing to capture her scent the same way he needed to ensnare her.

She jumped, springing back from him, a screwdriver clutched in her hand, fear making her eyes wide, her face taut.

He hadn't made a sound, so he knew she must have merely sensed his presence. "Sorry, I didn't mean to scare you."

She looked as if she might argue that and he noticed the signs of fatigue about her eyes. Amazing, it looked good on her, made her seem fragile and might make a man feel protective toward her.

"You could have said something sooner," she snapped.

He shrugged. "I didn't think you'd hear me over the radio."

Her look said she wasn't buying it. She seemed to be waiting for him to say something more.

She looked so innocent and sweet standing there in those awful baggy overalls, tendrils of her hair escaping her ponytail and cap to curl around that angel face. He could still smell her scent and didn't like the effect it had on him. The effect she had on him.

"I got a message. Something about my car?" he finally said.

Except for the fatigue and the obvious fact that he made her jumpy, she exhibited few signs she was under the kind of strain murderers often experienced. Or maybe she just hid it well.

"I took another look at your car," she said, avoiding his gaze as she hit a button on the pillar near her. The large overhead door on the second bay began to yawn open. "I was wrong about it needing parts." She bent back over the fender of the pickup. The tool clinked under the hood as she went back to work. "Your car's fixed," she said over the radio and the clanking of the garage door. "No charge. The key's in it."

"What?" He couldn't believe this. "Wait! One minute you need to order parts and the next you just fixed it?"

She continued working under the hood as if she hadn't heard him, but he wasn't leaving until he got an explanation. Not that he needed one. It was perfectly obvious, given what he'd done to the engine to start with. The car had never needed parts. She'd just said that to what? Keep him on foot? Keep an eye on him by having Emmett Graham chauffer him and report to her? Or call his bluff?

He stared at her behind. What he wouldn't give to see her without those baggy overalls. To see just how potent her powers over men really were. "Excuse *me!*"

She came out from under the hood slowly and turned to look at him, her eyes narrowing. "I fixed your car. There is no charge. What about that don't you understand?"

"Why you thought you had to order parts in the first place," he snapped.

For a moment, he thought she'd confront him about what he'd done to the engine. He welcomed it. It was time he turned up his investigation a notch anyway.

She locked eyes with him for several heartbeats. "I guess I made a mistake."

Like hell.

She gave him a well-what's-your-problem-now look, then turned back to her work.

What *was* his problem? *Her.* She'd erected a shell around her as cold and hard as this damn desolate countryside and he wanted to be the man to tear it down. He wanted to see some honest emotion in those brown eyes. It was high time this town knew the real Charlie she kept hidden the way she did her body beneath all those layers of baggy clothes. It was time to expose her to the world.

He grabbed her and spun her around. All he wanted was her undivided attention, to force her to look him in the eye, to see a glimmer of a crack in that shell. All he wanted was an honest reaction out of her.

He'd never planned to kiss her. Not even when his lips dropped to hers. But then it was too late. Her fragrance filled his senses as his mouth covered hers in a hard, demanding kiss. Her pupils widened only slightly as if the kiss hadn't been as much of a surprise to her as it was to him. Then his senses were filled with the tactile pleasures of her full, lush mouth, the warmth of her breath as she let out a whisper of a sigh and he felt her body tremble at his touch, her heart a hammer next to his.

"Charlie?" a male voice echoed through the garage.

Gus jerked back from the kiss, back from the madness. He stepped away, pleased to see emotion like golden sparks in the depths of Charlie's brown eyes.

Unfortunately, that emotion turned out to be anger.

"Don't ever do that again," she whispered hotly, sounding at least a little breathless. "Kissing me will get you killed." She stepped back over to the pickup as if nothing had happened. "Hey, Wayne! How ya doin'?"

Gus turned in the direction the voice had come from—the gaping open garage door—his heart still pounding from the impact of the kiss. Or maybe it was just from the stupidity of it. He'd only kissed one other woman he'd strongly suspected of murder—Natalie—and that had nearly gotten him killed. He hoped to hell kissing Charlie hadn't been the kiss of death.

A man with curly blond hair stood silhouetted in the garage doorway nervously fidgeting with his coat sleeve.

"I need to talk to you, Charlie," Wayne said, sounding upset as he looked from Charlie to Gus. "It's real, real important."

Charlie shot Gus a pointed look as she wiped her

hands on a rag. "Well, come on in, Wayne, and tell me about it."

Gus felt as if he should say something to Charlie, the kiss still coursing through his veins like a powerful drug. But what was there to say? How could he have forgotten that kissing her could get him killed—just as she'd warned him? Just as it had Josh?

That thought sobered him.

He stepped around her and the pickup, headed for the rental car, wanting to tell her that they weren't finished. But he figured she already knew that.

"What's up, Wayne?" Charlie asked. "You having car trouble again?"

Gus had just reached for the handle on his rental car's door when the sheriff's car pulled up outside, blocking his exit. A uniformed man got out and started toward them, shielding his eyes as he tried to see into the darkness of the garage.

Gus heard a sound behind him and turned to see Wayne disappearing through the back door, making a hasty exit.

"Bryan," Charlie said, nodding to the sheriff as he stepped into the garage. "What can I do for you?"

"Heard a knock in the engine on the way down from Libby. Thought you might take a look." The sheriff was gray-haired, probably in his sixties, possibly a contemporary of her father's. It was obvious he and Charlie knew each other and well. Another cause for concern.

"Sure," she said, sounding calm as hell. "Would you mind moving your car though so this fella can get out? He's anxious to be on his way."

Gus smiled at that as the sheriff went to move his car.

"Goodbye, Gus," Charlie said, turning her back on him.

He stared at her backside for a moment, disturbed that the sheriff's visit didn't appear to be causing her any concern at all. Was it possible, Gus wondered, that he could be wrong about her? Or was she just one cool cookie?

One thing was for sure, he thought, remembering the kiss. There was a hell of lot more to Charlie Larkin than he'd first thought.

"Charlie?" he said, realizing it was the first time he'd said her name.

She turned, seeming a little surprised herself.

Earlier when he'd grabbed her and kissed her, he'd just wanted to get a reaction out of her. Now all he wanted was to wipe out that unnerving calm composure of hers. He wanted her as off balance as he felt.

"That's something about Josh Whitaker having your locket on him," he said as he opened his car door and slid in. He smiled at her through the windshield as he closed the door and started the engine, her surprised expression what he'd hoped for.

He was betting few people knew about the locket being found on Josh. Gus couldn't imagine how Josh had come by it. But he'd lay odds Charlie knew.

As he backed out, she gave him a look that held a warning. Or was it a threat? Either way, he had her attention. And she looked anything but calm.

CHARLIE WATCHED Gus drive away, still fighting the disturbing effect of his kiss. She wanted desperately to blame it on the fact that it had been so long since she'd kissed anyone. Rather, since anyone had kissed her, she amended, afraid to think she might have kissed him back—even for an instant. She stood in the garage feeling weak and shaky, her heart still hammering, her lips branded with Augustus T. Riley's kiss. And now he knew about the locket.

Sheriff Bryan Olsen cleared his throat.

She looked up to find him standing with his hat in his hand, looking contrite, looking worried.

"That knock I said I heard in my engine," he said softly. "It was just pretense."

She nodded, having suspected as much. Bryan Olsen and her father had been best friends and she knew he thought it was his job to protect her. She wanted to unburden him of that task and had tried over the years, but she knew that Bryan would have walked through fire for her father—and now found himself in the middle of a firestorm because of her.

"There's been a leak about the locket," he said miserably. "I got a call from Phil Simonson not thirty minutes ago." He didn't need to tell her how incriminating it was to have her locket found on Josh Whitaker's body.

She could think of nothing to say.

"It's a murder investigation, Charlie, and I don't think I need to tell you that the fact that you knew him doesn't help matters."

She shook her head.

"It sure would help though if we knew how Josh Whitaker had gotten that locket," the sheriff said.

Her heart thudded like a death march in her chest

as she looked at him. He was trying to warn her. Had he found more incriminating evidence in Josh's car that would link his death to her? Or was he just worried, as she was, that it was only a matter of time before he did?

"I suppose Whitaker could have been poking around at the lake and just found the locket," he said.

They both knew what the odds of that were.

"But it doesn't explain what he was doing up here to start with," the sheriff ruminated. "It doesn't help either having Trudi going around telling everyone she saw you with Josh the day he disappeared." Bryan flicked his gaze at her. "She swears she saw you kiss him."

"I never saw Josh that day, so I couldn't have kissed him," Charlie said, reminded again of her most recent kiss.

"Well, I think we all know how Trudi is," he said.

Trudi had lied either for attention—or for Forest. Trudi and Forest had a history and might have been together today if it hadn't been for Jenny.

"Bryan, I told you that Josh and I didn't have that kind of relationship." They'd already been over this. She'd told the sheriff how she had met Josh when she'd volunteered on the help line in Bozeman. Josh had been starting a statewide help line and teaching volunteers.

Josh had been incredibly easy to talk to and she'd ended up pouring out her whole life history over coffee one night. They'd been friends. But that had been it. "I haven't seen him or talked to him in years."

The sheriff nodded. "Is there any chance he might

have forgotten you and that's why he didn't stop in when he came up here?''

She wanted to say yes, but she shook her head. She and Josh had been close. He was like the older brother she'd always wanted. ''We were friends. I don't think he would have forgotten. I think that's why he had the locket.''

The sheriff nodded. ''Yeah, the locket. So if he'd somehow come in possession of the locket, he would have tried to see you to give it back?''

''I guess so.'' Josh had known how she felt about Quinn, so she found that hard to believe. But since she'd told Josh everything, he might have thought the locket would give her some kind of closure. She couldn't imagine him driving all this way and not coming by. ''Maybe he never got as far as town. Maybe he went straight to the lake,'' she said more to herself than to the sheriff.

''To meet someone, you think?'' he said as he turned the brim of his hat in his fingers for a moment. He stopped as if an idea had just come to him. ''He didn't call you by any chance? Or you call him, say, from the pay phone outside?''

She stared at him, realizing this wasn't an idle question. ''He tried to call me at the pay phone?'' she asked in shock.

Sheriff Bryan Olsen looked down at his boots in answer. ''And someone called him from the same number.''

She had to fight to squeeze a breath out. ''It wasn't me, Bryan. I swear to you, I haven't spoken with Josh in years. I told you some man called the house, but I can't be sure it was even Josh.''

"Well…" He put his hat back on his head and stood looking down at her, worry in his gaze. Worry that he couldn't keep her safe? Or worry that she wasn't telling him the whole story?

"Why would I lie about him calling me?" she asked. "It doesn't make any sense."

The sheriff nodded. "Unless there was some reason you didn't want anyone to know you were talking to him."

Yes, that was exactly what it looked like. She felt sick.

"I'm just afraid all hell is going to break loose now that the Simonsons know about the locket," he said, obviously hesitant to leave her alone.

All hell had already broken out when Augustus T. Riley had come to town gunning for her.

"I'd just stay clear of the Simonsons if I were you," the sheriff said. "If there's any trouble, you call me."

She nodded, her heart a sledgehammer in her chest. The next time she saw Bryan it was more than likely he'd be stopping by to arrest her for the murder of Josh Whitaker and they both knew it.

He reached out to pat her shoulder, then put his hat on, turned and walked to his car.

She watched him leave. The moment he disappeared from view, she grabbed the top of the pickup's tailgate for support, her stomach roiling so badly she thought she might throw up. Someone was trying to frame her for murder. There was no doubt in her mind about that now. The locket had been planted on Josh to make her look guilty. The calls made from the pay phone outside the garage. But how had they even known about Josh? And where did the locket fit into all this?

At least she knew who had told the Simonsons about the locket, she thought, recalling Gus's parting words. Bryan said someone had leaked the information about the locket and Helen said Gus had asked Trudi directions to Phil Simonson's house after lunch—not long before the sheriff got the call about the locket.

Chapter Ten

Earlene Kurtz lived in a trailer on the north end of town. She opened the door in jeans and a large T-shirt, a spatula in one hand, her expression only mildly surprised to find Gus standing on her doorstep.

He recognized her from yesterday when she was at the wild-game processing plant working with T. J. Blue.

"My name is—"

"Gus," she said. "I know."

"Then you probably know why I'm here."

"You want to know about Charlie." She smiled and motioned him inside.

He stepped through the door, closing it behind him as she went into the kitchen where she was scooping dough onto a baking sheet. The trailer smelled of chocolate chip cookies.

"My son will be home soon. I always try to have a treat for him," she said, her back to him. "That's why I work the early shift."

He studied her. She was one of those women who carried her weight around the middle, giving her a square shape set on two legs. Her face was tight with the extra weight she carried. Her brown hair, long and dull, making her look older than he knew she was— a few years younger than Charlie.

"Would you care for a warm cookie?" she asked as she slid the new batch into the oven.

He shook his head and looked around. The trailer was an older model, but clean and neat inside. She seemed to do all right for a single mother. "I need to know about you and Charlie Larkin."

She turned to look at him. "We're friends." She shrugged as if that was the whole story. "Which most people don't understand, given the circumstances and who fathered my son."

"I heard Quinn Simonson fathered your son."

She nodded. "I was pregnant with Arnie when Quinn died."

"How pregnant?"

"Four months." She wiped her hands on a towel and glanced toward the living room. "You want to sit down?"

He pulled out a chair at the kitchen table and sat, trying to make sense out of this. Earlene was the reason Charlie and Quinn had gotten into a huge fight at Freeze Out Lake, the reason Charlie had refused to get back into the car that night and the reason Quinn had roared off—if not the reason he'd gotten killed.

"I guess I find it hard to believe you and Charlie are friends," he said at last. "I mean, I would think Charlie might be resentful toward you and vice versa."

"You don't know Charlie, do you," she said, making it sound as if he was missing something in his life because of that. "She hates it that Arnie doesn't have a father because hers meant so much to her. She's promised to teach him how to work on cars.''

"Do you see much of her?" he asked.

"She takes Arnie for me when I have to go to Libby or Missoula for something," Earlene said. "And we get together for lunch. She really loves Arnie. I think she's afraid that because he resembles Quinn he might grow up to be like him." She continued to stand, leaning against the kitchen counter, watching him.

"How did Quinn take it when he heard you were pregnant with his child?" Gus asked, wondering if she would have been showing at four months. Possibly not, given her size.

"He wasn't interested in being a father—let alone a husband," she said and smiled sadly.

"Maybe he would have changed his mind after you had the baby," Gus suggested.

"I like to think so. I loved Quinn. He was charming and cute and I'd always had a secret crush on him," Earlene said. "He told me he wasn't seeing Charlie anymore. I believed him. But it turned out that was a lie. Quinn lied about a lot of things."

Something in the way she'd said that… "You think there were other women?"

She smiled. "I'd bet on it."

"Did Charlie know about them, too?" he asked.

Earlene shrugged. "Maybe. But Quinn was pretty persuasive. I mean, he got Charlie up to the lake that night for the party, didn't he? He might have been able to talk her into coming back to him if Trudi hadn't announced to the world that her sister who worked at the clinic had told her that I was pregnant with Quinn's baby. Of course Quinn denied he was the father, but I think it was the last straw as far as Charlie was concerned.''

"Do you think she loved him?" Gus asked.

The timer went off. She picked up a hot pad and opened the oven. "You mean enough to kill him?" She shook her head as she pulled out the cookies, filling the room with the wonderful smell. "Charlie was going off to college that fall. She and Quinn had been *the* couple in high school but she'd broken up with him before the party. I think she knew he wasn't the guy for her. Not long-term. Quinn wanted his freedom, but he wanted Charlie, too, although looking back, I think it was Phil who wanted Quinn and Charlie together. Maybe he thought there was money to be had with the garage.'' She began to slip the cookies from the sheet to a wire rack with a pancake turner.

"So you don't think Charlie was serious about Quinn?" Gus asked, wondering why that pleased him when it took away her motivation for killing Quinn—if indeed he had been murdered.

"So why the big fight the night at the lake then?" he asked. Finding out Quinn had been cheating on her had to have made her angry. But angry enough to kill him if she didn't care that much about him?

"She was furious with him for bringing her up to the lake. I suppose she told you about the time Jenny almost drowned?"

Charlie hadn't told him anything.

"Charlie hates that lake and Quinn knew it but he still drove her up there against her protests," Earlene said.

If Charlie were that afraid of the lake, then would she lure Josh up there to kill him? "I'm sure you've heard about Charlie's bad luck with men," Gus said. "Any thoughts on that?"

She scooped the last of the cookie dough onto the baking sheet, her back to him. "Isn't it obvious? Someone in this town wants to hurt Charlie."

"Like who?"

She finished, slid the cookie sheet into the oven and set the timer before she turned around. "Trudi has always been jealous of Charlie. The Simonsons blame Charlie for Quinn's death." She shrugged.

"What about T. J. Blue and Rickie Moss?" he asked.

"I think they like perpetuating the idea that Charlie is cursed when it comes to men."

"There is no doubt that Rickie got cut that night on his date with Charlie, and T.J.'s trailer did burn down, right?"

She nodded. "But Rickie had tried to rip off some dope dealers a month before that. After his accident in the woods, he paid them the money he owed them. And T.J.? There are people in town who would tell you he set that fire to collect the insurance and started the rumor about the curse to shift the blame. It was arson but no one was ever arrested. T.J. collected the insurance and bought himself a cabin." She shrugged again. "So it all depends on who you talk to."

He could see that. "What about the Simonsons?" he asked. "Are they part of Arnie's life?"

She met his gaze. "What do you think?"

He thought Phil Simonson wouldn't acknowledge

his own grandson if it meant he might be expected to help with support. "Did you know Josh Whitaker?"

"No."

"He was the emergency room doctor on call the day you took Arnie to the hospital in Missoula for his asthma attack."

Earlene looked surprised. "Really? I don't remember him. I can't say I paid much attention to anyone but my son." She frowned. "I do remember the doctor being very kind and caring, though. I'm sorry I didn't remember his name."

Gus studied her for a moment, convinced she was telling the truth.

"Do you think Charlie had anything to do with Quinn's death?" he had to ask.

"If she did, I wouldn't blame her," Earlene said.

"But your son doesn't have a father."

She nodded and looked away. "No, he doesn't."

On his way out, Gus passed Arnie Kurtz, a towheaded seven-year-old with blue eyes. He looked enough like Jenny and Forest's little girl that they could be brother and sister. But he doubted Phil or Forest would ever let the two kids, so close in age, ever be friends. Some lines just weren't crossed.

As Gus neared his car, he wasn't surprised to see that he had company. "Hello, Sheriff. I was planning on paying you a visit."

Sheriff Bryan Olsen pushed himself off the patrol car he'd been leaning against. "Then my timing is perfect. Want to tell me what brings you to Utopia?"

Gus figured the sheriff already had a pretty good idea. "I'm just looking into Josh Whitaker's death for the family."

"Oh, really? I thought Josh Whitaker didn't have any family," the sheriff said. "Both parents deceased."

"I believe he has a half brother," Gus said.

"You know I don't think you're here on behalf of Josh Whitaker's half brother or any other member of the family," the sheriff said. "Your reputation precedes you, Mr. Riley."

Gus couldn't tell if that was good or bad.

"Word around town is that you've been asking a lot of questions about Charlie Larkin," the sheriff said, eyeing him. "Why is that?"

"She knew Josh Whitaker."

The older man nodded. "She told me all about that, but that doesn't mean she killed him."

Charlie had told the sheriff about her relationship with Josh Whitaker? "Then you know about the calls made to and from the pay phone outside the garage?"

"I received all of that information from the Missoula police," the sheriff said. "I'd like to know how you got the information, though."

Gus ignored that. "All the evidence in this case points to Charlie Larkin." He ticked off on his fingers. "She knew Josh, the calls were made from her pay phone, her locket was found on his body."

The sheriff's jaw muscle jumped. "All circumstantial." He pulled off his hat and seemed to study the brim for a few moments. "I've known Charlie Larkin all her life," he said slowly. "Her father was my friend. I'd stake my life on her being innocent of any wrongdoing, but I'm also a law enforcement officer, responsible for the lives of the people in this county. That's why I'm asking you not to get involved in my ongoing investigation. All things considered, it would be safer for everyone involved if you were to return to Los Angeles.''

Was there a reason the sheriff wanted him out of the way? ''Are you trying to run me out of town?''

''Just making a suggestion, Mr. Riley. You're smart enough to have noticed that any man who gets around Charlie Larkin seems to have bad luck. I don't think that's a coincidence. If I were you, I'd put a few thousand miles' distance between the woman and yourself. For your own good.''

''If you're so convinced Charlie is innocent, then who *is* killing and maiming these guys?'' Gus demanded.

''That's what we're trying to find out,'' the older man said.

''Not fast enough,'' Gus snapped. ''Thanks for the advice, Sheriff.'' He got into his car. In his rearview mirror, Gus watched the sheriff watch him drive away.

When he looked up, Gus realized he'd taken the wrong turn. The road wound around through the pines, passed some old logging equipment and a gravel pit. He was just getting ready to turn around and backtrack when he spotted two pickups parked on the far side of the gravel pit. Did everyone in this county drive trucks? It appeared so.

He recognized one of the trucks as Forest Simonson's about the same time he saw Jenny standing next to it talking to a man Gus didn't recognize until he had driven past. Both Jenny and the man had seemed startled to see a car as Gus passed. Startled and guilty-appearing. As the road curved, just before he lost sight of them, Gus glanced in his side mirror. Jenny Simonson was in T. J. Blue's arms. What the hell?

As Gus drove through town, he felt anxious. He'd spent the morning and part of the afternoon going over everything he'd learned from the time Josh Whitaker's body had been found. There was always a point in a case when he felt jumpy. When he'd found out enough that he wished he hadn't known the truth. He'd found out a lot about Charlie Larkin and yet he still had no proof that she was a killer. What evidence there was pointed straight to her, and all the good deeds she'd done couldn't change that.

So why was he having doubts? Because of some kiss? Or because of all her many loyal supporters and all her good deeds? Or because the people who professed her guilt all had an ax to grind?

He shook his head, realizing he wasn't basing those doubts on fact, but feelings. He'd been down that road before on the Natalie Burns case. Come hell or high water he wasn't going down that road again. The last thing he'd let himself do was get emotionally involved with Charlie Larkin and make the lethal mistake of trusting a killer again.

But he had to admit, he'd turned over a lot of stones and wasn't happy about most of what he'd found underneath. Like Jenny and T.J. He didn't even want to think about what Forest would do if he found out. *When* he found out.

Gus told himself it wasn't his problem. This wasn't his town. All he cared about was finding Josh's killer and then going home. Home. Los Angeles seemed like light-years away.

There had to be a way to flush out the killer—no matter who it turned out to be.

The problem was: Charlie had gotten to him. He didn't want her to be the killer.

He'd just found the road back into town, when an idea hit him like a two-by-four upside the head. It was crazy and way too dangerous for a sane man to even consider. But right now he was desperate and his sanity was in question because he was starting to doubt that Charlie Larkin had killed anyone—based on little more than a few nice stories about her and a damn kiss—and that was even more dangerous to his well-being than what he had planned.

CHARLIE WAS SITTING in the Pinecone, having a cup of tea with Helen when Gus walked in. She suddenly felt trapped, the air around her too dense to breathe.

His gaze fell on her and he moved quickly toward her as if he'd been looking for her. She felt her stomach lurch. What did he want *now?*

He slid into the booth across from her, smiling. "I've been looking for you."

That she'd gathered. "Are you having car trouble *again?*" She hadn't meant to sound so sarcastic.

His smile deepened. "We both know any trouble I've had has nothing to do with my car."

She stared at him, wide-eyed amazed that he would finally admit it—and here. Suddenly she was aware that, besides Helen, everyone in the café was watching them. And since it was coffee-break time in Utopia, quite a few locals were in the café, plus several of the worst gossips in town.

Gus reached across the table and took her hand in

his before she could draw it back. "I've missed you," he said loud enough that everyone had to have heard him. He turned her hand palm up and began to caress the sensitive skin with the pad of his thumb. "After that kiss earlier—"

His touch set off tiny jolts across her palm. She jerked her hand free. "I know what you're doing," she whispered hoarsely, trying to keep her voice down so the others couldn't hear.

He smiled, flirting, as he leaned over to brush a lock of hair back from her temple, his touch making her shiver. "I'm doing what any man would do under the circumstances."

"You're going to get yourself killed," she whispered fiercely.

"You don't have much faith in me," he whispered back. "If getting close to you will lure out Josh Whitaker's killer, then that is exactly what I'm going to do. Unless you know something I don't?" He grinned, his face just inches from hers.

From a distance it would appear they were locked in an intimate conversation—instead of an adversarial one. "I think it's high time someone tried to break that curse."

"This isn't about any curse," she hissed back. "This is about a book, the one you're planning to write about me."

He lifted an eyebrow. "Only if you turn out to be the killer."

"Please, Gus, don't do this," she pleaded, panicked. "You don't realize how dangerous it is."

"Oh, I think I do," he said, capturing her hand again in his. "You're trembling. What is it you're so afraid of, Charlie? That something might happen to me? Or that I might learn the truth?''

She stared at him, wanting to deny that she was responsible for any of this. But she couldn't. Because she had a terrible feeling that somehow she was responsible for all of it. As crazy as it sounded, there *was* a curse on her.

''I don't want to see you get hurt,'' she said, realizing that was true. He was the enemy. He'd come here to destroy her. But just the thought of the danger he was putting himself in—

''Do you have a better idea?'' He cocked his head at her. ''That's what I thought.'' With her hand still in his, he slid out of the booth and moved to her in a blink.

It was obvious he planned to kiss her again. She turned her head as he bent toward her. A soft chuckle emanated from deep with in him as he nuzzled her neck, brushing her hair back with his free hand.

''Mmm,'' he breathed against her bare skin. ''I love the way you smell.''

She felt goose bumps ripple across her skin as he trailed kisses down the column of her neck, finding a sweet spot between her neck and shoulder. A shaft of heat arced to her center, a sigh escaping her lips.

His chuckle this time was hoarse and she felt his breath quicken against her neck.

''Everyone in here is going to think we're lovers,'' she whispered breathlessly.

''Yes,'' he said softly into the hollow of her throat.

''We *aren't* lovers.''

''No,'' he said, letting go of her hair and drawing back. ''Not yet.'' He smiled as he cupped her chin in his warm palm and turned her to face him so quickly, too quickly to stop him. His mouth dropped to hers, stealing her breath, sealing the trap he'd just set for himself.

Then he was gone, whistling as he left, stopping at the door to grin back at her, aware everyone had seen. "See you later."

She watched him walk to his car. He turned as he reached it and grinned at her as if he'd known she'd be watching him. Damn him. She could feel his gaze, as hot on her skin as his kisses had been. Damn fool.

"What was that about?" Helen demanded as she slid into the booth Gus had just unoccupied.

"I wish I knew," Charlie said, surprised how breathless she was. Still. He made her feel things she'd never felt before. Damn him. Worse, it was just a game to him. All he cared about was catching a killer—and it was clear when the dust settled, he believed she'd be the one caught in his snare.

"Wow, he certainly has some effect on you," Helen said. "You should see yourself."

Charlie looked into the reflection in the café window. Her face was flushed, her eyes shiny bright. She looked like a woman who'd just made love with an exciting man. She touched her palm to her heated cheek and looked past her own reflection to see Gus back out and head south.

She watched him until the car disappeared down the highway. What did he plan to do now? And where was he going? There was nothing that way except— Her heart quickened as she realized where he was headed. Freeze Out Lake.

Chapter Eleven

Gus headed toward the lake. He'd set the stage and now had to play out his hand, no matter how it turned out. He reached into the bag on the seat beside him and pulled out the .38 special. He didn't have to check to see if it was loaded. He always kept it loaded on a case. He slipped it into the shoulder harness he'd pulled on before going looking for Charlie.

He told himself there was no reason to start looking over his shoulder just yet. Even with the small-town grapevine, it would take time for everyone to hear about him and Charlie. Not only that, no one knew he was going to the lake. He hadn't even known himself until he left the Pinecone and realized it was time he finally checked out the place that Josh had died.

He'd been putting it off. But knew he couldn't anymore.

He believed that Charlie was innocent. She couldn't have killed Josh. But someone had. Someone who wanted him to believe Charlie was a killer.

That's why Charlie's locket from Quinn had been found on Josh's body.

Someone else in this town had to have known Josh.

Gus couldn't be wrong. Not this time. What other answer was there? A curse? Or someone who didn't want Charlie to find happiness as Earlene had suggested? Neither wanted to fly, not when faced with the facts. Fact: Someone had murdered Josh. Fact: Josh had Charlie Larkin's locket on him.

He shook his head and concentrated on his driving, reminding himself of one of his first books. Her name was Natalie Burns and she was out on bond after being arrested for allegedly killing her lover. She was young and beautiful and Gus had been green and stupid. He'd bought into her innocence. And she'd tried to kill him.

He swore he'd never make that mistake again.

He hadn't gone far down the highway when he saw the sign to Freeze Out Lake. Slowly, he turned off, remembering how eerie it had been in the dark less than forty-eight hours ago. He had at least an hour before it got dark again.

The turnoff spot didn't look all that much better in the daylight. The snow had melted back where the weed-grown road disappeared into the trees. Even though it wasn't quite late afternoon, shadows hung heavy in the pines, making it hard to see very far up the road.

He didn't relish the idea of driving up there now. But he'd also never been one to back down from something just because it was hard—or unnerving.

Shifting the rental car into a lower gear, he started up the road to the lake, the tall weeds slapping the front fender and hood as he wound his way through the dark of the pines and up the mountainside.

He thought about the other men who had come up

this road and never lived to come back down it. The tracks through the weeds were still visible where the wrecker had brought out Josh Whitaker's body and car. He tried not to think about that.

The road was narrow and snowy in some places, muddy in others. He took it slow as he climbed higher and higher up the mountain, until at what seemed like the last moment, the trees opened and there was the lake.

He hit the brakes. For just a split second, he feared Charlie had done something to his car. Relief swept through him, making him almost giddy, when his brakes worked and he brought the car to a stop at the edge of the mountain lake.

The scene was beautiful in a creepy sort of way he couldn't explain. A perfect mountain lake surrounded by tall dark-green pines. Josh had died in this desolate place. The thought sent a chill through him hardening his resolve to see justice done—and at any cost.

He got out, surprised how cold it was. The water was clear, an icy-looking dark green. He stepped to the edge, knelt down and felt it. The water was warmer than he'd expected, as if it hadn't caught up with the change in weather yet.

Where had Josh's car gone under? he wondered angrily. Had Charlie been here? Had she watched it? Had she lured him up here? Someone had. It didn't make much sense for Josh to drive up here otherwise, not with the lake so far off the beaten path. Josh had been killed with a single blow to the back of the head with a blunt instrument. Had the killer been in the back of the car? Or had Josh been killed out here and then put back into the car before it was rolled into the lake?

Gus's blood ran cold when he thought that Charlie could have stood in this very spot and watched the car sink with Josh Whitaker in it. Another one down.

What had made Josh come up here? Who?

Too many questions and no answers. And so far, Gus reminded himself, he hadn't been able to find one piece of solid evidence that Charlie Larkin was responsible nor any solid proof that she was innocent either.

Suddenly he sensed rather than heard someone behind him. He whirled around going for his gun. Charlie stood directly behind him. A wrench gripped in her right hand.

"What the hell?" It came out on a breath, his heart lunging as he stumbled back into the water, almost falling on the slick rocks as he pulled the .38 from the shoulder holster and leveled it at her.

She stood with her arms at her sides, the wrench gripped so tightly in her fingers that her knuckles were white. She didn't move, didn't even seem aware of him as she stared out at the lake, her eyes glassy.

"What are you doing here?" he demanded and realized he was standing in six inches of water. He sidestepped her, getting back on dry land, putting a little distance between them. The damn woman had scared the hell out of him.

Why hadn't he heard her approach? His gaze flicked past her. Where was her van? He would have heard the van. Unless she hadn't wanted him to. Because she'd followed him here, her intention pretty obvious.

"What the hell were you doing sneaking up on me like that with a wrench in your hand?" His voice came out a rasp. The look on her face was freaking him out. "Answer me, dammit."

She seemed to shake herself out of a fog. Her eyes moved from the water to his face. She blinked, almost as if surprised to see him. But not nearly as surprised as she was when she looked down to see the wrench in her hand.

"Oh," she said and stuck the wrench back into a pocket of her overalls. "I didn't mean to scare you."

"Right." The same words he'd said to her earlier. What was this, payback? At least she wasn't still doing her zombie thing. Nor was he now floating facedown in the lake. Though that possibility didn't seem that far off.

"This place scares me more than it does you," she said, glancing at the gun in his hand and dismissing it.

He doubted this place scared her more right now. She could have killed him!

Her gaze went to the lake again. Her eyes widened as if— He swung around expecting to see— Hell, that was just it, he didn't know what he expected. Maybe some waterlogged, weed-covered dead body emerging from the deep.

But there was nothing. Just the last of the sunlight leaving a gold film on the surface. Not a whisper of a breeze in the pines. No sound at all. Except for the pounding of his pulse like surf in his ears.

He swung back around to face her again, feeling like a fool for turning his back on her. But she hadn't moved, hadn't gone for the wrench, hadn't taken her eyes off the lake, as far as he could tell. Her skin looked chalky and her eyes—those dark-brown mesmerizing eyes—seemed to be seeing something horrible that only she could see.

He recoiled at the thought, drawing back from her, realizing what she might be envisioning. Josh's car sinking into the eerie dark water.

He stared at her, not sure what frightened him the most. That he didn't want to believe she was a killer. Or that he couldn't get a bead on her, couldn't be sure of anything about her. Except for the fact that she scared him. Hell, he was still shaking from finding her standing behind him with that damn wrench in her hand. But when he'd set up this trap at the Pinecone, he'd known she might come after him and try to kill him. Just not this soon. He reminded himself that she hadn't tried to kill him. Yet.

"Charlie?"

Her pupils were dilated. Sweat had broken out on her upper lip. Her freckles practically jumped off her face. She began to sway.

He swore under his breath as he holstered the gun and caught her.

The moment he touched her, she blinked, then seemed startled to see him again. She righted herself, drawing back, as if afraid of him. What a joke that was. With relief, he watched her color come back, afraid of what he'd just witnessed, realizing just how much he didn't want her to be the killer.

"What was *that* about?" he asked. This lake was freaking her, that much was for sure.

A tremor seemed to quake through her. "I've only been up here one other time since—"

He thought she was going to say "The night I killed Josh Whitaker."

"—the day my friend Jenny almost drowned."

He stared at her, remembering what Earlene had told him about Jenny almost drowning and Charlie's fear of the lake.

She shifted her gaze to him. "Jenny Lee Simonson, now. We were swimming and she must have gotten a cramp—" She looked back out at the lake. "I swam to her and grabbed her arm—" Another tremor rattled through her. She hugged herself and looked over at him again, seeming a little embarrassed, definitely shaken. "I know it's crazy, but it almost felt as if someone, something, was trying to pull her under."

"You saved her life," he said, more to himself than to her. Another heroic deed. Or had she tried to kill Jenny as well? He felt as if he kept peeling away layers and still couldn't get to the real Charlie Larkin.

"How long ago was that?" he asked. "Before or after Quinn died?"

She looked at him, as if surprised he'd bring up Quinn. For a moment, he didn't think she'd answer. "Before. I didn't want to come up here that night with Quinn, but he—" She shook her head and looked away again.

"I heard he brought you up here to a kegger and the two of you had a huge fight that night."

"Is that what you heard?" She sounded tired and didn't even bother to look at him.

"Actually, I heard that you found out that he'd fathered Earlene's baby and you were angry. Angry enough to kill him?"

She said nothing and he wondered how far he

should try to push her, given where they were and the fact that she might have more than a wrench in the pockets of her baggy overalls.

"So what made you come up here today if you hate this lake so much?" he asked, figuring he probably wouldn't get an answer to this either.

"You." Her gaze swung to his, her eyes suddenly as dark and cold as the lake and just as hostile.

He felt a tremor of his own. "You followed me?"

She seemed to find amusement in that. "Haven't you been tracking me?"

He didn't answer. It surprised him now that she'd ever reminded him of Natalie. Charlie was much more complex, much more intriguing, much more dangerous. He'd never known a woman like her. And doubted he ever would again.

"After what you did back at the café, I couldn't let you come up here alone," she said.

"Oh, so you planned to *protect* me with that wrench, not knock me in the head and leave me floating facedown for dead."

She glared at him. "You really believe that I'm a killer? Did you know that Josh was deathly afraid of water? He almost drowned when he was young and he'd never been able to get over his fear."

Yes, he knew that. He thought of Jenny and her near drowning. He wondered if she'd gotten over it, wondering if anyone ever really did get over it. "So he'd have to trust someone implicitly to meet them here."

"I can't imagine any reason Josh would let himself be talked into coming up here. It had to be a matter of life or death."

"Seems it was. His death," Gus said.

She met his gaze. "You aren't taking this seriously."

"Oh, but I am."

"Not if you don't realize how dangerous it is for any man who gets too close to me," she said, her voice low.

"Right, the curse," he said. "How close did Josh get to you?" Silence. "Talk to me. What do you have to lose?"

"I could end up the subject of your next book."

"Only if you're the killer," he said and smiled. She would make one hell of a book.

"So tell me about you and Josh. I know he tried to call you before he disappeared last fall. Your name was also in an old address book of his."

"I'm impressed," she said.

"Don't be. I didn't even know you were a woman until the night before last at the garage."

She nodded and gave him a small smile.

He realized he'd never seen her really smile, but he would like to. "Then when Josh's body was found in Freeze Out Lake with your locket in his pocket…"

She blew out a breath. "All the so-called evidence led right to me."

"There's more. A doctor at the hospital overheard a phone conversation of Josh's just before he disappeared. The woman doctor said Josh was agitated and upset. When she asked him if anything was wrong, he said it had something to do with a friend. She got the impression it was a woman, a woman he was obviously worried about." He took a breath. "So you and Josh were...lovers?'' he asked, knowing he was going to hate her answer.

She cocked her head at him. "Sorry to disappoint you, Josh and I were just friends, but maybe the person who killed him didn't know that,'' she said. "Or maybe it was enough.''

He hoped his relief didn't show. She hadn't seduced Josh. Or at least that was her story. "So how did you meet?''

"We were both working on a help line and got to talking one night.''

"When was this?''

"Not long before I returned to Utopia.'' She made a face. "Don't look at me like I'm some sort of saint. I was volunteering for class credit in college. Josh, well, Josh had started the help line and was training volunteers. He really was something special.''

"This was in Bozeman then. I heard he was a hell of a nice guy,'' Gus said, trying not to let praise of Josh affect him the way it had for most of his life— negatively. "So you were *good* friends?''

She nodded. "What are you getting at?''

"Was he easy to talk to?''

"Yes. He liked helping people,'' she said. "It wasn't just me.''

Had Josh thought he was helping someone when he'd driven up to this lake a year ago?

"Did you tell him about Utopia and the people who live here?'' Gus asked.

She stared at him. "What does this have to do with—''

"Did you tell him about Quinn?''

"Yes, but—''

"Let me guess," he said. "You told him you felt responsible for Quinn's death."

"I *do* feel responsible for Quinn's death," she snapped. "After all, if he hadn't taken off from the party the way he did maybe he wouldn't have wrecked on the way down the mountain."

"You can't hold yourself responsible for his temper," Gus said. "Is that the only reason you feel responsible?"

"Isn't that enough? He died so young and he was about to be a father. He'll never know Arnie."

Nor would Arnie ever know his father.

She bit at her lip. "Have you seen Arnie? He looks exactly like Quinn did at that age."

Gus nodded. "That's why you help Earlene out with him? You realize, Charlie, you're almost too good."

"Don't make more out of it than it is," she said. "I like kids. Earlene's a friend."

"After she slept with your boyfriend?" He shook his head. She wasn't just too good, she was too naive.

"What's wrong?" she asked, eyeing him.

"Nothing."

She let out a sigh. "You're afraid I'm another Natalie Burns."

He blinked in surprise. Both that she knew about Natalie…and that she'd hit so close to the truth.

"It made national news, I read all the newspaper articles when I looked you up on the Internet," she said by way of explanation. "She almost killed you."

"You checked up on me?" If she knew about Natalie, then she'd done a lot of checking. Why? Because he scared her? Because she was guilty? Or because she really was innocent?

"You're surprised by that?" she asked, studying him.

"Everything about you surprises me," he said.

She looked past him, the last of the day's sunlight on her face, dusk settling in the pines.

He followed her gaze. "What is that?" he asked, seeing something in the darkness of the pines. A structure.

"The old Simonson lodge," she said, her voice a whisper, as if she was afraid someone would hear her.

"I want to take a look inside," he said. He saw her recoil at the idea of going up to the lodge.

"It's been boarded up for years," she said quickly. "I'm sure there's nothing in there. Just dust and spiderwebs and..."

"And memories?" he guessed.

Her expression gave her away. He glimpsed a vulnerability that under other circumstances would have made him soften toward her. "If you're afraid, I can go by myself," he said and walked over to his rental car to get his flashlight. He knew she'd come with him. But why? Because she worried that something would happen to him? Or worried about something he might find? "Coming?" One thing was for certain. He wasn't letting her out of his sight until they left the lake.

She fell into step beside him as he walked toward the woods, the beam of the flashlight trailing over the rocky shore as they neared the old lodge.

He stopped a few yards out to admire it, the walls constructed of hand-hewn logs, the foundation of rocks taken from the shoreline. She was right. It had been boarded up, but some of the boards were missing, others broken.

He climbed the steps to the porch, not surprised to find that someone had been here recently. The rusted padlock on the door had been busted. The door stood ajar.

He shone his light into the crack between door and jamb. There were dusty footprints on the old wooden floor. He pushed with one hand and the door creaked open.

A rustling sound came from deep within the lodge.

"It isn't safe," Charlie said and grabbed his arm. "Please."

He turned to look at her, her face pale in the glow of the flashlight, her eyes wide and frightened, and he remembered kissing her earlier, remembered the feel of her against him and was shot with an arrow of desire so strong he almost took her in his arms again.

He heard another noise, this time it sounded as if it was behind the lodge. Another limb cracked. He stepped around the edge of the porch to shine the light into the pines behind the lodge. It was getting darker, pockets of blackness had settled under the trees. The air seemed colder. His light picked up movement in the pines, something shapeless, the crack of dry, dead twigs as it moved away.

"Please," Charlie said behind him.

He turned to look at her again, the beam of the flashlight pointed at her feet. She looked scared and cold. He decided he'd seen enough. He could always come back up here and look around the lodge in the daylight. The thought had little appeal right now though. And what was the point? The tracks were probably the sheriff's when he'd searched the area for evidence.

"Okay, let's go," Gus said and shone the flashlight ahead of them as they left the lodge and walked up the shoreline to his car.

The surface of the lake mirrored the night sky. A cold silence seemed to hang over the place like an icy cloak and he was glad she'd talked him into leaving. He didn't like it here, didn't like thinking about the tragic things that had happened here. Josh had died here. That reminder hit him harder than he wanted to admit. Hurt him more. Normally, it took a lot to scare him. But he felt anxious and would have sworn they were being followed.

He saw Charlie glance back, pretty sure she sensed the same thing. He turned and shone the flashback back along the shoreline. The light skittered over the rocky shore, across the silky green of the dense pines, glowing for a moment on the weathered boards of the Simonsons' old lodge, but found nothing else in the darkness.

Was it the lake? Or was it knowing Josh died here? Or was it being with Charlie that had him jumping at his own shadow? he wondered as they reached his car.

He looked over at her, half expecting her to pull a real weapon from those baggy overalls and kill him. He wondered how long it would take someone to find his body. Especially if she weighted it down with rocks.

The problem was, she looked a hell of lot more frightened than he felt. Could he be wrong about her?

She scared him. But was it because she was a killer? Or because he was afraid of falling for a woman who could break his heart? Or worse?

He glanced toward the rental car, suddenly worried she might have done something to it before he'd found her standing behind him. "You need a ride back to town?"

She shook her head and looked at him as if there was something more she wanted to say. Or do. "I have my van up the road."

"Any reason you didn't drive it down here?"

"I was afraid I'd get stuck."

He hadn't thought about getting stuck when he'd pulled up so close to the water.

"At least let me give you a lift to your van," he insisted, thinking about what Phil Simonson had said about her refusing to get into Quinn's car that night, the night the car crashed and Quinn was killed. "It's getting too dark to walk."

She glanced toward the deep pines back by the lodge as if she'd heard the sound again. Something was definitely out there. An animal? Or the real killer? Then she looked at the rental car. "All right."

Relieved they were both leaving, he opened the passenger-side door for her. She seemed nervous, he thought when he got in. She kept looking out into the trees as if afraid of what was out there. He kept thinking about the grizzly that had killed those campers. About the person who'd murdered Josh.

He couldn't see anything in the dense pines as he drove back up the road, the headlights illuminating only a narrow swath of overgrown-weed road in front of him.

Her van was right where she said it was. He pulled up next to it, and for a moment he thought she wasn't going to get out and he knew if she didn't pretty soon, he might be tempted to touch her—worse, to take her in his arms and kiss her.

"I wish you hadn't done what you did back at the Pinecone," she said, not looking at him. "I'm afraid for you."

"Just worry about yourself, Charlie," he warned her.

She shook her head, her eyes suddenly gleaming with unshed tears as she looked at him. "You're still convinced I'm a killer. Funny, but when I get around you, I *do* have the urge." She climbed out without another word, slamming the door behind her.

He watched her walk around the front of the car to her van, then reached over and notched up the heat. Sometimes he acted like a jackass, he thought as he waited until she got into her van. She motioned for him to go first. He shook his head and motioned that he would follow her. She didn't seem happy about that, but took off down the mountain ahead of him, her taillights glowing bright red.

He lost her partway down. Probably because she was driving so much faster than he was. Also because he was busy concocting a second assault as part of his original plan as he drove.

Sometimes he had to be as cold-blooded as the killers.

Chapter Twelve

The moment Charlie lost sight of Gus's headlights behind her, she pulled off onto a logging road and cut her lights to wait for him to pass.

Then she doubled back up to the lake. She'd heard the movement in the pines near the lodge and suspected it wasn't a wild animal. The only predator around here that stalked human prey was human.

She could see part of the lake, the surface glassy. Knowing someone had been out there watching her and Gus, was probably still watching her now, turned her blood to slush. Where was the person now? *Why not finish what you started?*

She knew the answer, just as she knew that the person in the woods had killed Josh and would kill Gus if he didn't get out of town and soon. What she didn't know was why. Or who hated her enough to do this to her.

Angrily, she pulled out her flashlight from the glove compartment and got out. "Come and get me, you coward, you crazy bastard," she said to the thick darkness of the trees. Silence answered.

She listened, hearing nothing but the thudding of

her pulse in her ears. Whoever was after her wasn't through making her suffer. She avoided the lake, cutting through the pines to the lodge, just wanting this finished now, before Gus could be hurt. She didn't want his death on her conscience, too. But she knew her feelings when it came to Gus were much more complicated than that.

The lodge stood silhouetted against the night sky. She shone the light on the weathered siding, finding the door. It stood open, just as Gus had left it. Again, she listened, but heard nothing except her own heart now a steady drum in her chest.

Slowly, she climbed the porch steps, her courage faltering at the thought of going inside. She wondered how many girls had lost their virginity in this musty old lodge. How many in particular lost it to Quinn Simonson.

She shoved the door open a little farther and shone the flashlight inside. The beam trailed over the worn wooden floor to the fireplace, following a set of footprints in the dust. Someone had definitely been here— and recently. There was burned wood in the old fireplace and a spot that looked as if someone had lain down a blanket in front of the fire.

She'd caught a glimpse of something on the lodge floor earlier with Gus. Now she found it in the beam of her light. Cautiously, she stepped inside the room, the smells taking her back to a time she didn't want to remember. Her light picked up the object again. She moved to it and reached down to pick up the toy from the floor where it had been dropped. It was a small yellow metal pickup truck.

She turned it in her fingers, shining the light on it,

trying to remember where she'd seen it before. Earlene's little boy, Arnie. He'd been playing with it the last time she'd seen him a couple of weeks ago. She was sure it was the same toy truck because it had looked old—just like this one.

She put the toy in her pocket and turned with the flashlight, suddenly wanting out of here, wanting to be far from this lake, far from this place where two men she'd known had died. She didn't want to think about how the toy had gotten here. Or why she'd felt such a need to come back for it.

A movement in the doorway caused her to swing around, her heart lunging and a scream catching in her throat as the beam of the flashlight fell on the dark shape of a man.

"Oh, you scared me half to death," she cried, the flashlight beam wavering in her hand as the light fell on Wayne.

He stood in the doorway, both hands buried deep in the pockets of his coat, his expression sullen. "I saw you with him," he said, sounding funny.

She didn't need to ask what he'd seen or with whom. It was clear he was upset about seeing Gus kiss her earlier in the garage. "What are you doing here?" she asked, trying to keep her voice light.

He didn't answer, just stood glowering at her, and she realized with a jolt that he was angry.

"You shouldn't be here," he said morosely. "It isn't safe."

She told herself she had no reason to fear Wayne. But before this moment, she hadn't realized he could be jealous of her. She tried to hide her anxiety. "I was just leaving. Do you want to walk me to my van?''

He didn't answer. Didn't move.

''I better get home,'' she said too brightly. ''Aunt Selma will be waiting for me.'' She stepped toward him, afraid he'd block her way. Her hand dropped to the pocket of her overalls. She felt the cold steel of the wrench and prayed she'd never have to use it against Wayne. ''Did I tell you Selma loved the apples and pumpkins? She's making a pie for dinner tonight.''

He blinked, his expression a little less hostile. ''What about the squash?''

As she neared the door, he moved aside to let her pass. Relief swept through her, making her weak. She stepped out into the night, her flashlight beam bobbing ahead of her across the porch. She wanted to run, but didn't dare. What was Wayne doing here?

''Selma baked one of the big squash last night,'' she said as she walked down the shoreline, even though it was the longer route back to the van. But she felt safer out in the open than in the woods, and knew it was nothing more than an illusion.

Had it been Wayne she'd heard earlier when she was with Gus here at the lodge? She told herself Wayne wouldn't hurt anyone, that Wayne couldn't have found out about her friendship with Josh or been able to lure Josh to the lake—let alone kill him.

But right now, she couldn't be sure of anything. Right now, all she hoped to do was reach the van safely.

Wayne trailed along beside her, still obviously angry, judging from his brooding expression. She knew he must have a flashlight, but he didn't use it, just kept his hands buried in his coat pockets. What else might he have in there besides a flashlight? she wondered. A weapon?

As they neared her van, she saw his car parked just up the road. It couldn't have been him earlier. Unless he'd moved his car after Gus left, after she headed back to the lodge.

"Why don't I follow you," she suggested. "In case you have any trouble."

He looked over at her. "You are awful nice to me."

"You and I are friends," she said.

He nodded, biting at his lower lip, his gaze dropping to his boots. "I don't like him."

Gus. "He's leaving town soon," she said, hoping it was true.

Wayne certainly didn't look convinced.

She glanced pointedly at his car. "I'll follow you." Then she opened the van door, almost expecting him to stop her. Out of the corner of her eye, she saw Wayne move toward the old Chevy.

Her heart was hammering against her ribs as she climbed into the van and watched through the windshield as he walked to his car and got in. A moment later the lights flashed on and the Chevy began to pull away. She let out the breath she'd been holding.

Tears rushed to her eyes. Until that moment, she had refused to admit how frightened she'd been. Now she shook from the fear and relief. She'd known Wayne her whole life. Did she believe he was capable of murder?

As the Chevy disappeared down the road, she

leaned over the steering wheel and tried to stop shaking, no longer sure what she believed.

After a while she became aware of the cold. She lifted her head and looked around, surprised how dark it was, and reached for the key. She couldn't wait to get out of here, suddenly desperate to get home, needing the warmth of the old farmhouse, the familiar smells, the comforting sounds of her mother's and aunt's voices, the feeling of being safe, even if it was a lie.

As she drove down the winding mountain road, the pines thick and black on each side, the sky starless, she kept expecting to come around a corner and find a dark figure standing in the middle of the road.

When she finally hit the highway, she turned toward Utopia, with panicked relief. Only a few more miles.

But as she came around a corner in the highway, she spotted a vehicle pulled off on the edge of the pavement and recognized it as Wayne's Chevy. She slowed, letting her headlights illuminate the vehicle. The right rear tire was flat, the car at an angle as it leaned toward the ditch.

For a moment she thought about not stopping. But as she stared at the car, she remembered what Wayne had said earlier in the garage about needing to talk to her. She'd completely forgotten about that and obviously so had Wayne. Why had he hightailed it out of the garage when the sheriff had arrived? Was he in some kind of trouble?

She realized he could have followed her to the lake to talk to her. To tell her whatever it was that had been so important. But when he'd seen her with Gus at the lodge, he'd probably completely forgotten about it. That would be like Wayne. Better than believing he'd had anything to do with the "accidents" involving the men around her.

She flipped on her brights as she pulled closer, expecting to see Wayne hunkered down beside the car in the weeds trying to change the tire in the dark.

An uneasy feeling came over her as she stared at the empty space beside the flat tire. Rolling down her window, she called out, "Wayne?", thinking he might have gone into the trees for some reason.

No answer.

Maybe he didn't have a spare and had walked into town. It wasn't that far, especially if he cut through to his mother's place.

A limb cracked in the trees off to the left. "Wayne?" She felt the hair stand up on the back of her neck as she stared blindly into the darkness. But why wouldn't he have waited, knowing she was behind him?

Earlier she'd been ready to face whatever was after her, just wanting it to be over. But now she wanted out of here. She didn't want to think about the toy she'd found or what it meant, any more than she wanted to think about Wayne and what he'd been doing at the lake.

She rolled up the window and locked the doors, all the time telling herself she was acting ridiculous. Probably just a wild animal this time.

She stopped at the garage to call the sheriff on the pay phone and told him about seeing Wayne's car. Bryan promised to check on him. As she started back toward the van, she stuffed her cold hands into her pockets, felt the toy truck. Her thumb ran along the side of the metal. It was old. Had it been Forest's or Quinn's? Is that why it was in the Simonsons' lodge? But she was sure she'd seen Arnie with the toy.

The county road was coming up in her headlights. Just a half mile on up the road was Earlene's trailer. It wouldn't take but a minute to stop by her place.

EARLENE WAS SURPRISED to see her. "You're just in time for dinner."

"Thanks, but I'm headed home. You know Selma, dinner will be ready and waiting." Charlie picked Arnie up as he came running out from the rear of the trailer. "You get bigger every time I see you. I have something of yours," she said, putting him down. It always jolted her, the fact that he was the spitting image of Quinn at that age.

She pulled the tiny yellow toy truck from her coat pocket and held it out to him. The boy frowned and looked to his mother.

"That isn't his," Earlene said, her voice tight.

"Are you sure? I thought I saw him playing with it the last time I was over," Charlie said, feeling the tension, but unable to understand what was wrong here.

"It's Skye's," Earlene said.

Skye Simonson? "Jenny's daughter's?"

Earlene nodded. "It belonged to Quinn." She looked over at her son. His eyes welled with tears, his lower lip quivering. "Arnie took it from Skye at school when he heard it was Quinn's. I made him return it."

Arnie had taken the toy that had belonged to his

father. "When was that?" Charlie asked, still worried why it had ended up at the boarded-up Simonson lodge.

"A couple of weeks ago right after that day you were here," Earlene said, drawing her son to her, her hands on his narrow shoulders. "Where did you get it?"

"I found it at the old lodge at the lake," Charlie said.

Earlene nodded and looked away. Charlie guessed that was where she'd lost her virginity to Quinn Simonson as well. The man was anything but imaginative.

"I wonder how it could have gotten there," Charlie said, putting the toy back into her pocket. "I'm sorry I thought it was Arnie's."

"No problem." Earlene smiled. "Sure you don't want dinner?"

Charlie felt better by the time she turned onto the county road. A mile and a half later, she pulled up in the front yard of her family's farmhouse, not bothering to put the van in the garage out back by the barn, just glad to see the lights on inside the house, warm, welcoming. Safe.

As she got out, she smelled snow in the air and knew it would be falling again within hours. It made the evening seem colder, definitely darker, and she remembered that Selma was making pot roast for dinner. Her favorite. Suddenly she felt as starved as if this might be her last meal.

As she opened the back door, she wondered where Spark Plug was. He usually met her at the door. She stepped into the kitchen and was hit with the wonderful aroma of pot roast and garden vegetables and pumpkin pie. She shrugged out of her coat and started to hang it on a hook by the back door. Her hand froze, all her fears coming back in a sickening rush.

Mingling with the wonderful smells of supper was another familiar fragrance—one that balled her stomach in a knot. The distinct aroma of Augustus T. Riley's aftershave.

The realization had only just hit her when she heard the unlikely sound of his laughter. The aftershave she could easily have conjured from memory since she'd smelled it on her skin ever since their last kiss. The scent was haunting.

But not the laugh. It was rich and deep, lyrical and not at all what she would have expected from him.

Then she heard her mother's high voice and the spell was broken. She rushed into the living room to find Gus sitting in her father's chair, Spark Plug lying at his feet. That dog had never liked any man other than her father.

And Spark Plug wasn't the only one who Augustus T. Riley had charmed, it seemed. Vera's cheeks were flushed with excitement, her eyes brittle bright. She laughed at something Gus said, her laugh painfully pure and sweet. Even Selma, it appeared, wasn't immune. She sat next to Vera on the love seat, also smiling at Gus.

He looked up, the first to see Charlie. Something in his gaze changed in a blink. It became cold and calculating, the humor leaving his face. And yet he smiled. "Why, here she is now," he said and got to his feet. Spark Plug lifted his head, but didn't bother to get up.

"Isn't she just lovely?" her mother said.

"What are you doing here?" Charlie demanded without thinking.

Her mother looked startled then disapproving. "Why, he came by to see you, dear," she said. "I've invited him to join us for dinner since it sounds as if he'll be staying in town for a while."

Selma looked surprised by her niece's behavior as well as she got to her feet. "Speaking of dinner—" She moved to Charlie, touched her arm as she headed toward the kitchen. "Help me, will you, dear."

"Is there anything I can do?" Gus asked from behind them.

"No," Charlie said without turning to look at him. "You've already done enough."

Once in the kitchen, Selma turned to stare at her "What in heaven's name—"

"I don't like that man," Charlie whispered angrily. That was putting it mildly. "He has no business here."

Selma's eyes widened. If her aunt had The Gift, then why hadn't she recognized this man for what he was: a wolf in sheep's clothing. "For heaven's sake, why not? He seems perfectly charming and quite taken with your mother."

Charlie groaned inwardly. "Believe me, it's all an act. The only thing he cares about is getting me."

Her aunt raised an eyebrow. "*Getting* you?"

She shook her head. Now wasn't the time and what was she going to say anyway? She took a breath. "I was just surprised to see him here, that's all." The last thing she'd expected was for Gus to show up at the house. But she guessed she should have known that trying to warn him off wasn't going to work. How far did he plan to take this?

She shot a glance toward the living room where he was visiting with her mother and suddenly felt afraid of what her mother might say and Gus might believe.

When she looked back, she found Selma eyeing her intently. "He is a very attractive man."

Charlie looked at her askance. "You aren't trying to fix me up, please."

"Maybe I still notice a good-looking man when I see one," Selma said, getting her back up. "Can you say the same? When was the last time you spent some time with an attractive man? Maybe tonight will do you good."

Charlie wasn't about to get into this now. "What can I do to help with dinner?" She just wanted this over with as quickly as possible.

"Go change into something more…appropriate. I think we'll eat in the dining room. Your mother would like that."

"Why don't we break out the best china?" Charlie said sarcastically. "Or have you already put that in my hope chest?"

Selma made a face. "I don't see why you're so upset. He said his business was going to keep him in town for a while and he'd forgotten something he wanted to ask you, so he stopped by. It seemed like the polite thing to do, asking him to dinner."

His business was keeping him in town, was it? *She* was his business. And who knew what he planned to ask her now.

"He's just having dinner with us, Charlotte,"

Selma chastised. "I can't see what that could hurt. You know how your mother loves company."

Charlie nodded, feeling trapped.

"Unless there is something I don't know." Her aunt left the statement hanging.

"I thought you knew everything?" Charlie said, only half-joking. How could she tell Selma that this man had come to Utopia to destroy her without telling her everything else? Worse, he'd just invaded her last stronghold: her home. And now he'd discovered her Achilles' heel: the two people she loved most in the world, Selma and her mother.

"I'm not young enough to know everything," her aunt said, stealing a line from Oscar Wilde. "But I do know he's interested in you. He could be just what you need."

Right. "It's only dinner," Charlie said to herself, wondering how she'd get through it. She could hear her mother's laughter. She didn't want to leave Gus alone with Vera a minute longer. "I'd better get changed."

When she came back down in a loose-fitting, long-sleeved forest-green corduroy jumper, her aunt gave her a disapproving look. It was the least formfitting clothing she owned—other than the overalls she worked in.

"Isn't she just lovely," her mother said. But her mother always said that when she saw her.

Charlie could feel Gus's eyes on her and finally looked directly at him. He smiled as if amused that she would try to hide her body from him any more than she would try to hide any other truths about herself.

Dinner was a nightmare. Her mother told embarrassing stories about Charlie's childhood. Gus urged her on, no doubt taking it all in to use against her. Selma, thankfully, tried to steer the conversation to other topics—such as Augustus T. Riley himself—and it would work for a few minutes before Vera would remember something else funny to tell about Charlie.

Gus laughed at all the stories, along with her mother. He would glance over at Charlie occasionally, his gaze always calculating, as if trying to see under her skin.

"So what brought you to Utopia?" Selma asked him between her mother's stories.

He smiled and chewed a bite of roast beef as he studied Charlie. "I suppose I can tell your aunt the truth." He took his time, chewing, swallowing, all the while watching her. "I'm a writer," he said as if confessing something Charlie didn't know, his gaze shifting to Selma. "I travel around looking for interesting stories, something out of the way, unusual." Sounded innocent enough. Unless you knew the truth about Augustus T. Riley's books.

"Utopia is out of the way," her mother said gaily. "And unusual, I suppose. Isn't it, dear?"

"I'm sure there are a lot of other places that are more out of the way and unusual than Utopia," Charlie said, pretending more interest in her pot roast than him.

"I can't imagine that anyplace could rival Utopia for its uniqueness," he said, a smile in his voice. "I'm fascinated. In fact, so much so that I'm considering doing a story on Utopia's female mechanic. I want to know everything about her, as long as it takes.''

"Oh, isn't that wonderful!" her mother cheered. "We must show him all the photo albums."

Charlie choked on the bite she'd taken.

Gus quickly poured her more water. "Are you all right?" he asked, sounding concerned.

He wouldn't want her to die, she thought angrily. Not until he got his book—and saw her behind bars.

"Fine," she managed to say. "And what if I don't want a book written about me?" she whispered fiercely so her aunt and mother couldn't hear.

He smiled. "I think we both know the answer to that one," he whispered back. Raising his voice, he said, "I'd love to see your photo albums of Charlie."

"Maybe some other time," Charlie said, looking pointedly at her aunt.

Selma got to her feet. "Your mother would like ice cream with the pumpkin pie I made for dessert—"

"I'll get it," Charlie said and got up so abruptly she almost spilled her freshly refilled water glass. But she had to get out of the room, and the freezer was out in the shed behind the house. The cold snowy night was just what she needed.

She didn't even take her coat, just rushed out the kitchen door and across the yard, bucking snowdrifts, to the shed. Spark Plug trailed behind her, obviously trying to make up for being a Judas.

Charlie noticed that Gus had parked beside the barn, his car hidden from view of the road. Had he purposely wanted to surprise her when she came home by hiding the car? She wouldn't put anything past him.

Once inside the shed, she leaned against the closed door and took long breaths, trying to calm herself. Her body vibrated with the familiar fear. He'd as much as told her she was his next book. His next female murderer.

But hadn't she known when he'd come into the garage two nights ago that he was after her? She closed her eyes, feeling the tears, warm on her cheeks. She didn't want to see anyone else get hurt. Especially Gus. But how could she stop him?

Something bumped against the outside of the shed. Her eyes flew open but she didn't move, didn't even breathe. Spark Plug began to growl low in his throat.

Chapter Thirteen

Gus wondered if she was going to come back. He listened, half expecting to hear her van engine as she left. But she lived here. Where could she go?

He glanced across the table at her mother. No, Charlie couldn't leave her mother. Nor her aunt. They obviously depended on her. And if Charlie had ever planned to run, he suspected she would have done it a long time ago.

But she was gone long enough that he was beginning to have doubts.

"I think I'd better see if I can help, Charlie," he said, excusing himself. He walked to the back door and opened it, expecting to find her on the porch, avoiding him.

The sky had turned to a satin gray, the fallen snow reflecting upward to make the night not quite as dark as it had been. He could feel tiny snowflakes and see his breath coming out in white puffs.

He stepped to the edge of the porch. There were tracks in the snow leading to the shed and the stand of pines beyond. "Charlie?" That's when he heard the dog growling. He couldn't see Spark Plug, just hear him, a low rumble of a growl coming from the outbuilding. "Charlie?"

Just before he reached the shed, he saw something large move away from the dark side of the building. At the same time, the shed door flew open and Spark Plug came barreling out. The dog's growl turned into a bark as a shadow sprang into view and took off toward the pines.

Gus started to go after the dog and the retreating figure of a person, but Charlie came hauling out of the shed just then, brandishing a shovel, the blade catching the snowy light.

"It's me!" he called out before she could level him with it.

She stopped, silhouetted in the otherworldly gray light, the shovel raised above her head, then she stumbled toward him, dropping the tool in the snow.

He caught her, pulling her to him awkwardly. "Are you okay?" He could feel her trembling in his arms. Just the fact that she had seemed glad to see him was enough to make him wonder if she was all right.

She nodded against his chest and took a shuddering breath. Even in the dim light from the open door of the shed he could see her dark eyes and the fear lodged there.

Spark Plug ran back from the pines. From the distance came the groan of an engine, the sound dying off as the vehicle left. A pickup in need of a muffler. Much like the one that had driven by Murphy's last night when Trudi had come by.

"Who was that?" he asked.

She shook her head and stepped from his arms.

"Look, I can tell you're scared. Talk to me. Tell me what's going on."

She glanced toward the trees where the figure had disappeared. "I've been trying to tell you but you haven't believed me. Someone is trying to frame me for Josh's murder." Her gaze came up to meet his. The look in her eyes made him weak. Just like the sweet warm feminine scent of her.

He wanted to believe her. Oh, at this moment, with her so close, he definitely wanted to.

"That person will try to kill you next," she said.

"Not if I find him—or her—first."

She shook her head and smiled ruefully. "Is it really worth it? Risking your life for a stupid book?"

"It's more than a book," Gus said evenly.

"Bull," she snapped, the word sounding alien on her lips. "You're dead set on me being your killer so you can write another book about a woman who murdered her lover. That is what you do, isn't it? Go after women killers."

"I do find them the most…intriguing," he admitted.

"Except Josh wasn't my lover and I didn't murder him," she said angrily. "But what do you care about the truth or about Josh Whitaker." She started to turn back toward the shed, but he grabbed her and jerked her around to face him again.

"I care. And it's more than a book to me. A hell of a lot more. Josh was my brother."

She stared at him in surprise. "I'm sorry. I didn't know he had a brother."

Gus nodded and looked past her to the snowy darkness. "He was my half brother. Our mother remarried after my father died. Josh and I weren't—'' he stumbled on the word ''—close. I was the black sheep of the family and Josh was—'' He glanced at her. ''Well, Josh was like you. Damn near a saint.''

She jerked free of his hold. ''Josh was a good man who cared about other people,'' she said defensively.

''Yeah, and that's probably what got him killed.''

''Too bad you're not out looking for the killer instead of trying so hard to pin this on me,'' she said. ''Your mind is already made up about me, isn't it?''

Not hardly, he thought. In fact, the more he learned about her, the more confused and uncertain he became. And he hated it.

''Okay, let's say someone found out that you knew Josh and got him up here to frame you for his murder,'' he said, thinking what a long shot that would be. ''How did that person get the locket Quinn gave you?''

Her eyes glistened. ''I haven't seen that locket since the night I threw it at Quinn seven years ago at Freeze Out Lake.''

''Could Quinn have picked it up?''

''I don't know. I threw my locket at him and went for a walk I was so angry with him. I suppose anyone could have picked it up.''

He sighed. ''What about Quinn's death? And Rickie Moss's accident and T.J.'s fire?''

''I didn't hurt anyone,'' she said, sounding tired, ''but I don't expect you to believe that. You'd already made up your mind that I was guilty before you even hit town, didn't you?''

He flinched at the truth in her words. ''You have to admit you were the likeliest suspect.''

"Exactly. Doesn't that make you just a little suspicious?"

Admittedly, it did. But she was right. He'd made up his mind about her before he'd even known Charlie was a *her*. He had wanted to nail Charlie Larkin for Josh. For himself because he hated to be proven wrong. Because he owed his brother. But that was before he met her. Before he had kissed her.

He glanced toward the trees, wondering about the person he'd seen run off. He doubted Charlie went after just anyone with a shovel. Nor did he question the fear he'd seen on her face. He wanted more than anything to prove her innocent. And it scared him.

She looked past him, toward the house, as if she'd heard something, and immediately stepped away from him.

He followed her gaze and saw the small form of her aunt come out onto the porch.

"Charlie?" Selma called. "Is everything all right?"

"I just couldn't find the ice cream," she called back. "We're coming." She turned to get the ice cream from the freezer in the shed.

"Let me do that," he said quickly and stepped into the outbuilding. It was dark except for a small nightlight on the far wall. Beside it was a large chest freezer. He opened it and spotted a carton of vanilla ice cream.

She still looked scared when he came back out and he felt a rush of doubt. What was she so afraid of? The truth coming out? Or was there really someone after her?

For just a moment he felt guilty for forcing his way

into her life. For relentlessly going after her with one single-minded intent: proving she'd killed Josh.

"If you let me, I might be able to help you," he heard himself say.

"We both know you didn't come here to help me. Just the opposite." She turned and walked away from him. It was clear she was sorry she'd fallen into his arms.

The dog came up and touched his hand with a cold nose. He bent down to pet Spark Plug, watching Charlie follow the narrow snow trail back to the house and the light.

He felt conflicted, unsure of himself, something he hated. It scared him. He feared being suckered in by another femme fatale. And yet, he could never have imagined anyone like Charlie Larkin and just how tempting it would be to believe her.

He and the dog followed her back to the house. She was standing in the kitchen digging in the silverware drawer when he walked in. Her cheeks were flushed from the cold, her eyes bright. She was trying hard to pretend that nothing had happened out by the shed and he wondered what she'd feared most: whoever the dog had been growling at or those few moments when she'd dropped her defenses with him.

"Let me at least scoop the ice cream," he said, watching her, fascinated and feeling an even stronger compulsion not only to believe her, but also get closer to her, closer to the truth—not to nail her but to free her. She was even more appealing here in this house, in her home, with her aunt and mother, and this sudden urge to protect her made him weak with desires that scared him.

He could see her getting ready to argue. "You can dish up the pie," he told her, "while I do the ice cream." He looked up at Selma who stood watching them both from the doorway, suspicion and worry in her gaze. "We'll bring dessert right in."

Selma nodded and with obvious reluctance left them alone in the kitchen.

"I like your aunt and mother," he said to Charlie as he moved to her side and took the ice-cream scoop from her still-trembling fingers.

She dug in a silverware drawer again, this time coming out with a knife. "Only because you think you can use them," she said, brandishing the knife.

He smiled and stepped back, pretending she and the knife frightened him. She frightened him all right, but not that way. "I'm not here to hurt anyone, just get to the truth."

"I wish I believed that," she said and glanced toward the other room where her aunt and mother were talking quietly, then at him again.

"Haven't you heard that the truth will set you free?" he asked, only half-joking.

"Then you should be out looking for a murderer," she said. "Not here scooping ice cream." She set about cutting the pie, lifting out portions onto plates as if at home in the kitchen as she was in a garage.

He scooped ice cream onto each of the plates with the warm pumpkin pie, wondering how he'd ever be able to eat pumpkin pie again without associating that cinnamony smell with Charlie Larkin.

She licked the side of her finger where she'd spilled a little of the pie filling.

He watched her tongue flick out and slide along

her finger, her eyes coming up to meet his. Desire burned through his veins hot enough to burn down the house.

She dropped her gaze and turned away to wash her hands at the sink, her back to him.

He took a breath and let it out slowly, remembering her in his arms, wanting to kiss her again, only this time for an entirely different reason.

"You sure you don't need help in there?" Aunt Selma called.

"No, I think we've got it," he said. Charlie still had her back to him. She shut off the water and made a project out of drying her hands before she turned. Her cheeks were flushed, but the kitchen was hot.

He took two pieces of pie and ice cream into the dining room.

Vera brightened, clapping her hands lightly at the sight of the pie and ice cream. "I love pie."

He put one down in front of her, the other in front of Selma, who was eyeing him hard.

"What kind is it?" Vera asked, staring at the plate as if she'd never seen pie before.

"Pumpkin," he said, and heard the back door open and close. "Charlie, I can take the ice cream back out to the freez—"

"I just put it on the porch for now, it's plenty cold out," Charlie said behind him, surprising him. She hadn't wanted to go back out to the shed. Not that he could blame her. But it still surprised him. She really was afraid of whoever the dog had been growling at.

He tried to tell himself that she might have been meeting someone out by the shed, someone she hadn't wanted him to see and the whole shovel thing might have been a distraction to throw him off, but even he couldn't make himself buy that story.

She put one of the servings of pie and ice cream in his spot at the table and, with hers in her hand, sat down again, smiling at her mother. "I think Selma outdid herself this time, Mom."

"Selma, did you make this?" Vera asked incredulously. "I didn't know you could cook."

A strained silence fell over the table as Gus pulled out his chair and sat down again. "This is the best pumpkin pie I've ever had," he said after one bite. It was the truth. He looked up to see Charlie looking at him as if everything out of his mouth was a lie. "I mean it. This is…amazing." He took another bite, watching Charlie. "It's good with ice cream, too."

She took a bite as if she was also enjoying it. He liked watching her eat. Hell, he liked watching her do most anything. She couldn't have killed Josh or anyone else. But he knew what he based that on had nothing to do with facts or evidence.

"I can't eat any more," Vera said, sounding tired. She pushed her nearly untouched plate back.

He finished the last bite of his pie and ice cream and put down his napkin. "Thank you for a wonderful meal and delightful company." He let his gaze move from Vera to Selma to Charlie where it lingered. "Let me at least help with the dishes before I leave."

"That is very kind of you," Selma said. "But unnecessary."

"Yes," Charlie agreed. "It's getting late. I'm sure you'll want to get back before the roads get any icier." She pushed to her feet and looked pointedly at him. "Good night, Mr. Riley."

"Gus."

She raised an eyebrow. "I thought it was Augustus T.?"

He smiled. She's the one who had everyone in this town calling him Gus, as if she didn't know. "Gus to you." A look passed between them.

"I think I'm going to bed," Vera said, rising unsteadily to her feet. "I don't know why I'm so tired."

"It's the weather," Selma said, quickly getting up to assist her. "Winter always makes you a little tired."

"Does it?" Vera frowned, then smiled at him. "Thank you for the pie. It was delicious. Imagine a man baking pies." She chuckled as Selma took her arm and they started across the room. "Burt can't boil water. I hope you didn't let him help with dinner. Has he gone out to put away the ice cream?"

"Yes," Selma said. "That's where he's gone all right."

"He's so good about doing for me," Vera said, a smile in her voice. "I'm lucky to have a man like him, aren't I?"

"Yes, you are," Selma agreed as the two disappeared into a room that had obviously been converted into a bedroom off the living room. Gus could see two twin beds and knew that Selma slept in the same room as her sister. That meant Charlie's bedroom was upstairs. Obviously, Vera couldn't be left alone.

"You were leaving?" Charlie said behind him.

"Some type of dementia?" he asked quietly, turning to look at her.

She waved a hand through the air and looked away, biting her lower lip for a moment, her eyes suddenly brimming with tears. "Alzheimer's." She looked so vulnerable, so devastated by her mother's disease, he wanted to take her in his arms and try to soothe her pain. But he knew he would only add to it, because he couldn't stop trying to find Josh's killer. If she was guilty. That damn "if" had only become bigger.

She walked to the back door, opened it, holding it for him. "Good night, Mr. Riley."

He followed her. "Gus." He could smell the scent of her soap still on her skin. Her gaze locked with his for a few precious seconds, then she looked away.

"It's getting late."

He nodded, knowing that leaving might turn out to be the only smart thing he did all tonight.

She found his coat and handed it to him. "Be careful, Gus."

"You, too." He shrugged into the heavy coat, not wanting to leave her alone here, alone with her mother and aunt who would be of no help if that person out by the shed came back. But he couldn't stay, even if she would have wanted it. He felt off kilter, confused and aroused, scared for himself, scared for her. This book—and catching the killer— meant everything to him, didn't it? He owed it to Josh. He'd failed Josh in life. He couldn't in death.

He stepped through the open door into the cold darkness. "Good night, Charlie." He picked up the ice-cream container and took it out to the shed, then walked through the snow to his rental car.

The engine started with a few coughs and groans. He wondered what the temperature was outside. Colder than he had ever been. The seat under his butt felt like a block of ice. He let the car engine run for a few minutes, a cloud of white exhaust billowing up behind it as the defroster went to work, blowing cold air up through the vents.

He wiped the condensation from the windshield with one of the gloves he'd purchased along with the coat and saw Charlie watching from the kitchen window. He thought of her mother and aunt, and the way she was with them. Feeling himself weaken toward her, he swore. Forgetting for even a moment that Charlie was a murder suspect could prove fatal. Natalie Burns had taught him that in spades. Only, Charlie was nothing like Natalie.

The defroster cleared enough of the windshield that he could see to drive. He shifted the car into Reverse. Charlie was still watching from the window. Reluctantly, he backed out, a desire to prove Charlie Larkin innocent ringing like a liberty bell in his head.

CHARLIE WAITED until Gus finally left, driving off in a fog of cold air, taillights disappearing into the trees that lined the snow-covered narrow gravel road out to the county road and eventually the highway and town. Then she grabbed her coat and headed for the trail she'd taken last night into town.

In her flashlight beam, she found the boot tracks in the snow. It was impossible to tell whether the person who'd been by the shed tonight had been a man or woman from the footprints. The ones heading toward the house were closer together; the ones leaving obviously someone running.

She walked to the nearest road, found the tracks where the person had parked. From the tire tracks, the vehicle had been a pickup. She looked down the road, seeing nothing but darkness and the deeper black of pines silhouetted against a starless sky. For two nights now, Spark Plug had chased someone away. Both had left in the same pickup, one with a loud muffler. Forest Simonson drove a pickup with a bad muffler. But most of the men she knew drove trucks that could use a new muffler. Blame Montana winters.

What had the person in the pickup wanted? Just to harass her? Or had they been looking for Gus? The thought gave her a twinge because tonight his car had been here.

She headed back toward the house before she was missed and had the dishes done by the time Selma came into the kitchen.

"I got Vera down," her aunt said, pulling out a chair at the table.

Charlie could hear the exhaustion in her voice. "You can't keep doing this."

Selma looked up, surprised.

"I've been thinking," Charlie said, softening her tone as she pulled up a chair across from her aunt. "We're going to need to get someone to come in and help with Mother soon, so why not do it now?"

Before Charlie could finish, Selma was already shaking her head. "We're doing just fine."

"I'm worried about you. I'm amazed how strong you are and how capable you are at your age—"

"Don't start with that age stuff."

Charlie reached across the table and placed a hand over her aunt's. "You know what I'm trying to say."

Selma looked up, her eyes bright with hurt. "That you don't think I can keep up my end."

"You know that's not what I'm saying. I'm wor-

ried about you. About..." She looked past her aunt
to the window where she'd watched Augustus T.
Riley drive away. "If something should happen and
I wasn't here to help—"

"I don't want to hear that," Selma said, pulling
her hand free.

"Maybe you'd better hear it," Charlie whispered,
remembering this was the second time in two nights
that someone had been outside the house. The evidence against her seemed too great. And she didn't
believe for a moment that the person trying to frame
her for Josh's murder was going to stop.

"Things have a way of working themselves out,"
Selma said, straightening her back before rising from
the chair. "It's not like we could find someone to
come in and help anyway. Not out here in the sticks."

Charlie started to argue, but Selma cut her off.
"We're both tired. I'm sure we'll both feel better after
a good night's sleep," her aunt said.

What Charlie wouldn't give for one.

Her aunt touched her shoulder as she went by on
her way to bed. "No more talk about getting someone
in. You know your mother wouldn't like that."

After she left, Charlie thought about Gus. She felt
torn between worrying about his safety—and worrying what he'd do next.

She stared out into the night, afraid.

GUS FOUND HIMSELF thinking about the stories he'd
heard at dinner, especially those about Charlie and her
dad. It was obvious Charlie had idolized her father
and spent many hours with him at the garage. Gus
could understand now why she'd become a mechanic
and stayed in this town.

He couldn't help but admire her obvious loyalty to her family. It was clear she would do anything for them. That's why it was hard for him to imagine her doing anything that would jeopardize that close relationship. And that realization was playing havoc with his thoughts.

He tried to concentrate on the narrow snowy road as he left the farmhouse. He'd never driven in snow before.

Ahead, a sharp curve cut into the side of a hillside. The road rounded a corner above the creek. Of course there was no guardrail. Nothing between him and the snowy rocks in the creek but air. On top of that, the packed snow was shiny slick.

He took his foot off the gas, afraid he was going too fast for the corner, and touched his brakes.

The moment his foot hit the brake pedal, he knew. An image of Charlie Larkin flashed in his head. My God!

He pumped frantically at the brakes for a few heart-stopping moments, panic completely obliterating common sense. Too late, he thought, to downshift.

The road turned, dropping off to the left in a steep incline that ended in the rocky creek below. He turned the wheel and felt the back end of the car begin to come around. He overcorrected as the car began to slide toward the edge of the road. It veered the other way, toward the hillside. The back of the rental car slammed into the embankment. The car spun the other way, toward the drop-off and the creek.

The left back tire dropped over the side of the road first. Gus watched in disbelief as he and the car went over the edge.

Chapter Fourteen

Charlie heard the whine of the siren and bolted upright in bed. She couldn't be sure if she'd actually been asleep. Or if she'd been lying in bed awake, waiting.

She scrambled out of bed, following the faint shrill cry to the window on the north side of the room. Even from here she could see the flashing lights through the trees and knew whatever had happened, happened at the curve.

Hurriedly, she dressed, trying hard not to let her mind get too far ahead of her. But fear constricted her throat and the pounding of her pulse in her ears drowned out everything except the sound of the siren. Her heart hammered so hard she thought it might kill her. Actually welcomed such relief.

But as she started the van, she knew dying would be the easy way out—and there was no easy way out of this.

Long before she reached the curve, she saw the lights of the sheriff's car blocking the road. She pulled the van over as much as she could without getting off into the ditch and the deeper snow. Then she got out and walked toward the curve, trying to see past the flashing lights of the patrol car to the activity beyond.

"Hold up there," a uniformed officer said as she approached. She recognized him right away. It took him a moment. "Ms. Larkin," Fred Mitchell said and seemed to relax. She'd met him when he'd come in the gas station with the sheriff asking about Josh Whitaker a year ago.

"I saw the lights from my house." Did she just feel guilty or was he looking at her as if questioning her story? "The siren woke me. What's happened?" Her heart was lodged in her throat.

"There's been an accident," Fred said. "Car went off into the creek."

She nodded, having known that's what it had to be. "Anyone hurt?" Her voice sounded strained, hoarse, scared.

"Wasn't a fatal. I think the guy was just shaken up, but the ambulance is running him to the county hospital in Libby just to be safe."

The night air suddenly felt too rarefied. She hugged herself, sucking in large gulps.

"Are you all right?" he asked, reaching out to take her elbow.

She nodded, tears stinging her eyes as she fought hard not to cry. "I think it might have been someone I know. A man who had dinner at my house earlier tonight."

"According to his driver's license, his name is Augustus T. Riley," Fred said.

"Oh" was all that came out. Her body had begun to vibrate.

"Looks like he was going too fast and slid off the curve. Not the first time it's happened on this stretch of road. I'm sure it won't be the last. The guy probably wasn't familiar with winter driving, being from California and all."

She nodded, her teeth chattering.

"Nothing you can do here," Fred said as he let go of her elbow and eyed her closely. "You should get home before you freeze to death. I'm sure your friend will be just fine."

Gus wasn't her friend. Far from it. She nodded, and turning, started back toward her van.

"Oh, by the way," he called after her, "the wrecker is hauling the car to your garage for now until Mr. Riley can decide what he wants done with it. There wasn't much damage considering it slid down that embankment and landed in the creek."

"Thanks." She didn't turn around. She just kept walking, slogging through the snow, her body aquiver with the now too familiar terror. Gus had gone off the road not a mile from her house. What was the chance it was an accident?

She drove back to the house, knowing she wouldn't be able to sleep the rest of the night but having nowhere else to go.

She climbed the stairs silently, not wanting to wake her mother or aunt. All she could think about was Gus. Thank God he hadn't been killed. Not even hurt badly.

Why hadn't he listened to her? She'd tried to warn him. She was shaking from a mixture of fear and relief.

The worst part was, she feared this close call

wasn't going to dissuade him. No, quite the opposite. If she knew Augustus T. Riley the way she was beginning to, this would only make him more determined. But what if it hadn't been an accident? Wasn't that what had her so frightened?

Before dawn, she dressed in her overalls and drove to the garage. The van's headlights shone on Gus's rental car where the wrecker had left it outside the garage.

Charlie parked and, taking the flashlight from her glove compartment, got out and walked toward the car. A steely-gray sky hung over her. Snow blanketed the town as deep and cold as the intense silence. No lights shone at any of the other businesses. No sound. No cars on the highway. She was completely alone, just as she knew she would be.

She slowed as she neared the car, her mind racing with possibilities. Something easy. Something obvious. Cutting the brake line. Or disabling the steering mechanism. Something that would survive the crash. Something that would come back to haunt her.

She shone the flashlight under the car. There was a long, wide scrape along the skid plate where the vehicle had slid over the rocks in the creek. She stepped closer, then knelt down to look under the engine to the brake line. Her heart began to pound. She gripped the flashlight, but her hand trembled so hard the light bobbed. She steadied it long enough to confirm her worst fears.

Her legs suddenly wouldn't hold her. She fell back in the snow, oblivious to the cold or wetness, and put her head down on her knees. Any investigator would see the cut brake line and know immediately Gus's crash wasn't an accident.

She could replace the brake line. It wouldn't take her any time. The sheriff wouldn't even question the tracks around the car. She could just tell him that she'd taken a look at the car. Even that wouldn't be unusual since it appeared she could get it running again and save the rental agency from having it hauled back to Missoula.

No one would have to know. Except her.

She could feel the sky lightening around her. If she was going to do it, she had to do it now. *Fix the line. Save yourself.*

GUS HAD BEEN WAITING in the cold for so long, he'd convinced himself Charlie wasn't coming and was starting to feel guilty about hiding out here with a camera and binoculars. He hadn't realized how badly he didn't want her to show up until he'd spotted the van's headlights and was filled with an overwhelming sense of regret.

But there she was and too early to have come to open up the station. Charlie had gone right to the car and shone her light under it as if she'd known that the brake line had been cut, something Gus had discovered earlier.

He didn't want to believe she'd had anything to do with his accident. But then, what was she doing here before dawn? Had she expected the wreck to be more dramatic, any evidence against her destroyed? No one would have questioned the accident in that case. Just a California boy driving off a snowy county road.

And here he'd been waiting and hoping it had been

the trespasser the dog had chased off who'd cut his brake line.

He feared the truth was staring him in the face. Charlie was here. Why? What was she going to do about the cut break line?

He felt sick. If she'd cut the line, the only way she could hope to get away with the act now would be to fix the brake line before anyone saw it.

He watched her through the binoculars from his hiding place, the camera with the telephoto lens next to him. Neither the binoculars nor the camera had been easy to come by in the town of Libby after he'd checked himself out of the hospital last night. But desperation often made things possible.

Charlie slowly got up from the snow. It would be light soon. Why didn't she get moving? If she was going to cover her tracks, she didn't have much time before this Podunk town woke up.

She turned off the flashlight and walked slowly through the semidarkness of predawn toward the garage.

Gus stomped his feet trying to warm them. Even with all the winter gear he'd had to purchase at Emmett's store, he was cold. And disappointed.

Why didn't she step it up a little? Was she so confident that no one would suspect her that she would tamper with evidence in broad daylight?

The thought gave him a twinge as he remembered what Trudi had said about no one believing anything bad about Charlie Larkin.

A light came on in the gas station office, then in the garage. Come on, Charlie. His feet were freezing. He didn't know how long he'd been watching his wrecked rental car, how long he'd been waiting for her. He was cold, and right now he just wanted it over.

When she came back out with her tools to cover up her crime, he'd get her photograph. Isn't that what he'd wanted? Some hard evidence against her. If she'd tried to kill him, then there was more than a good chance she'd killed Josh. Gus knew he should be elated. He'd been right about her from the first.

Hadn't he suspected she'd cut his brake line the moment he touched his brakes and the pedal went clear to the floorboard? And yet there still had been that instant of disbelief. Not Charlie. Not the Charlie he'd come to know.

He stared at the light burning in the gas station office, waiting for Charlie to come out with her tools to fix the brake line, wishing she would surprise him as she'd done so many times over the last couple of days.

So where the hell was she?

CHARLIE STOOD in the doorway between the office and the garage bays, struck with the oddest sensation that if she looked, she would see her father standing by the tool bench, a cup of coffee in his hand, waiting for her to show up so he could talk about the latest job.

He loved being a mechanic, compared it to being a detective. Each car came in with a mystery, most too easy for his years of experience, but every once in a while he would get one that challenged him. Those he loved and he would talk about them for days after, the way cops talked about tough cases they'd solved.

She could almost feel his presence, the feeling so strong she would have sworn she smelled the strong coffee he loved to drink.

With great pain, she shifted her gaze to look toward the tool bench, afraid she'd find his ghost standing there, afraid she wouldn't.

The spot where her father stood was empty.

Tears sprang to her eyes, a combination of relief that she wasn't losing her mind and unbearable disappointment. Right now, there was no one she would have loved to have seen more than her father.

There'd been days when she'd felt his presence in the garage, that presence so strong she'd almost turned to him, to ask his advice, or to tell him about a recent job she knew he'd enjoy hearing about. But none of those times had been as strong as this morning and she knew why.

She closed her eyes, aware of the lightening sky outside, the passing of time. But she felt no urgency because she knew she wasn't going to fix the brake line. She had never planned to. Couldn't. And the reminder of her father only made her more aware of that.

She opened her eyes, the sky a light silver outside the windows. Another day. Gus would be getting out of the hospital. He'd be coming back to Utopia, back to destroy her with a vengeance.

She turned away from the empty bays and stepped back behind the counter in the office. Josh had been murdered and now the brake line had been cut on

Gus's car. Since Quinn's death, any man who got close to her only got hurt—or killed.

Gus was still alive. Maybe if she acted quickly— She picked up the phone and dialed Sheriff Bryan Olsen's number.

"WHAT THE HELL?" Gus swore as he watched Charlie on the phone inside the garage office through his binoculars. Now didn't seem like the time to call anyone.

She hung up, but still didn't come through the door with her tools. Was it possible she wasn't going to fix the brake line? A surge of hope flooded him. Was it possible she hadn't cut his brake lines?

Ten minutes later, the sheriff's car pulled up in front of the garage. Charlie came out of the gas station office, locking the door behind her. The sheriff had gotten out of his vehicle and walked over to the wrecked rental car. He crouched down to inspect under the car. Charlie joined the officer.

It appeared she was pointing out the cut brake line. "What the hell?" Gus whispered, his breath frosty white, and found himself grinning.

He put the camera and binoculars in his bag and walked across the street to join them as the sun topped the pines.

"What's up?" he asked.

Charlie didn't seem all that surprised to see him. "You seem to be all right," she said, sounding anything but concerned about his welfare.

"Just a little banged up," he said. "Nothing to worry about."

She met his gaze, definitely not looking worried.

Instead, she appeared angry with him—as if this were his fault.

The sheriff straightened to full height. "It appears your brake line was cut," he said to Gus with a sigh. "Charlie called to tell me a little while ago. Any idea who might have done it?"

Gus glanced over at Charlie. She was looking at him as if she expected him to denounce her. "No idea at all," he said, turning back to the sheriff. "I'm sure Charlie told you about the trespasser on her property last night."

The sheriff gave her a surprised look. "No, as a matter of fact."

She was shaking her head. "I checked out the tracks. Could have been just about anyone in town wearing snowpacks and driving a pickup with a bad muffler."

The sheriff wagged his head and looked at Gus again. "I'll get the forensics guys over here but I doubt we're going to find anything on the car that will help us. I can also send them over to the house."

"I wish you wouldn't do that," Charlie said. "It will only upset my mother and aunt, and I assure you there is nothing to find."

The sheriff didn't seem pleased. "Okay, Charlie, if that's agreeable with Mr. Riley. He's the one who ended up in the creek."

Gus shrugged. "I trust Charlie's instincts on this."

The sheriff looked at him as if he'd lost his mind. Or another valuable body part. "I've got some more bad news," he said to Charlie.

She didn't look as if she needed more bad news right now.

"It's Wayne Dreyer," the sheriff said kindly. "He was killed last night. I'm sorry, Charlie, I know he was a friend of yours."

Charlie turned white as a sheet. Gus started to reach for her, sure she was going to collapse. But she seemed to find some inner strength and remained standing.

Gus remembered the young man who'd come into the garage yesterday and caught them kissing. "What happened to him?"

"He had an accident last night," the sheriff said. "After I got your call, Charlie, that you'd seen Wayne's car on the side of the road south of here with a flat, I rang his house. His mother said he was fine, heading back to change the tire. I got another call, a wreck between here and Libby so I didn't hear about Wayne until later. The jack must have slipped out while he was changing the tire. Happened about eight-thirty. A trucker found him pinned under the car just a little after that."

All Gus heard was the time of the accident. He'd been with Charlie at her house having dinner with her mother and aunt from eight-twenty-five. Charlie had a damn good alibi for this one—him. If it *was* an accident. It seemed too much of a coincidence that one minute Wayne was desperate to tell Charlie something and the next he was crushed under his car.

Gus looked over at her, anxious to get her alone. She'd told him last night that she thought someone was trying to frame her for Josh's murder. He had a bad feeling the murderer was getting tired of just trying to frame her. Gus was afraid Charlie would be the next victim.

Chapter Fifteen

Charlie just wanted to be alone. Wayne was dead. He'd said there was something important he needed to talk to her about. He'd been acting strangely at the lake last night and now he was dead. Another accident.

"We have to talk," Gus said the moment the sheriff left.

"Not now," she said, moving past him toward her van. The day had broken gray, no sun, the air heavy with the promise of snow, the trees stark against the silver sky. It matched her mood.

He grabbed her arm and spun her back around. "Yes, *now*. I'm worried about you."

She'd been angry with him from the moment she'd seen him come out of his hiding place earlier. "Do you think I don't know what you were doing across the street this morning?" she snapped, breaking free of him.

He held up his hands in surrender. "You had the chance to fix the brake line and save yourself and you didn't. I had to know."

She could only shake her head at him. "I didn't fix the brake line. What does that prove?"

"It just confirms what my instincts have been telling me."

She raised an eyebrow. "Your instincts?" She'd thought they'd gotten a little farther than that last night, but obviously she'd been wrong. "And what are your instincts telling you now?"

"I was wrong about you originally," he said, the words seeming to come hard to him. "I'm sorry."

She eyed him suspiciously, knowing it must be hard for him to trust—given what had happened on the Natalie Burns case. Last night when his brakes had failed, he must have thought she and Natalie were a lot alike—both having tried to kill him.

But she couldn't help being angry. And hurt. "If you expect me to jump up and down with joy at that news, I'm sorry to disappoint you." Last night she'd let herself believe he really wanted to help her. More than that, she'd felt a connection between them. It had been so strong that—

She shook her head, wondering what she'd been thinking. She and Gus weren't just from different worlds, they were from different planets. Los Angeles, California, and Utopia, Montana. Light-years apart. Just like what she and Gus each did for a living.

"So what has changed?" she asked.

"You. That is, not you, but the way— What I'm trying to say is that you aren't what I expected." He reached out to cup her cheek with his gloved hand. "Charlie, I care about you. I want to help you."

She drew back, out of his reach. "I don't want to talk about this, not now." She felt too raw. Too much had happened. Josh's death. Now Wayne's. And worse, she felt responsible for both.

"You're not responsible for what happened to Wayne," Gus said as if reading her mind.

Her head snapped up as her gaze met his. "But you suspected I was, didn't you?"

"I suspect everyone," he said, sounding angry, but with himself, not her. "It's what I do. I can't let myself trust a suspect."

"And that's what I am, isn't it? A suspect."

"You were and maybe you still are to the sheriff, but I don't believe you killed Josh. I know you couldn't have killed Wayne because I was with you at the time of his death." His gaze softened. "I don't believe you could hurt anyone."

She looked into his handsome face, her heart a dull ache. She could see what it had cost him to say those words, to trust again. She didn't want him to trust her any more than she wanted him to kiss her again or take her in his arms and tell her everything was going to be all right. Because she knew it wasn't.

She closed her eyes, unable to look at him without weakening. "Gus, someone cut your brake line."

"And I'm going to find him."

Slowly she opened her eyes. "If he doesn't find you first."

Gus smiled. "You keep underestimating me."

No, she thought, not in the least. Maybe that's why her heart always beat a little faster around him, the air seeming to crackle with expectation, the world more intense when he was near her. She'd known right away that he was dangerous. But she hadn't known just how dangerous.

"I hate that you're risking your life to find the killer," she said angrily. "It's senseless. It won't bring Josh back. Nor will it clear your conscience."

"Don't you think I know that?" he asked through clenched teeth.

"Then why not walk away now while there's still time?" she pleaded. "The sheriff will catch the killer. You'll get the justice you need. And you'll write other books."

He grabbed her upper arms and pulled her to him. "You think I could walk away now? Knowing someone is trying to frame you for murder? Knowing the way I feel—" His lips dropped to hers.

It was almost impossible not to lose herself in his warm mouth, in the full firmness of his lips, in the whisper of his breath.

She dragged herself away, heart pounding. "Please, Gus." She felt tears rush into her eyes. She couldn't even be sure what it was she was pleading for.

He shook his head. "Let me help you."

She stared at him, finally admitting to herself what she wanted—the very last thing she should want from a man like Augustus T. Riley.

"I don't want your help, Gus. I certainly don't want you risking your life on my account. Now, please, just leave me alone." She turned her back to him, felt the burn of tears. Damn him.

"Where are you going?" he asked behind her.

"Home."

She got into the van and drove down the street, refusing to look back at him. She hoped he would give this up, save himself. She couldn't bear the thought of him being hurt. Or worse, killed. And yet, the only way she could hope to stop him was to walk away from him.

GUS WANTED to kick something. He watched Charlie leave and swore under his breath. At least she was headed home. Her aunt and mother were there. She'd be safe. He hoped. Last night, someone had come to Charlie's yard to cut his brake line. Would they dare come back in broad daylight?

The killer appeared to be after Charlie's boyfriends. Not her. Jealousy seemed the obvious answer. But, if Gus was right, it had all started with Quinn's death, so revenge could be the motivation as well. Between the two, he could come up with a handful of suspects including Trudi, T.J., Rickie, Forest, Phil and Earlene.

As he watched the van turn off on the county road and disappear, he couldn't shake off the feeling that time was running out. That he had reason to be fearful for Charlie.

He stood for a moment, unsure what to do next. Eventually, the killer would come after him again. Not Charlie.

As he started across the street, he heard the sound of a pickup with a worn-out muffler coming up the street. He turned, expecting to see Forest Simonson's pickup. It was a dark color, just not the same dark color as Forest's. The pickup pulled into a space in front of the Pinecone Café and T. J. Blue got out.

Gus decided it was time to have breakfast. He got the new four-wheel-drive rental car he'd picked up in Libby and drove down to the Pinecone, remembering that the pickup he'd heard last night leaving Charlie's had had a loud muffler. And so had the pickup he'd seen drive by Murphy's that night Trudi stopped by.

SPARK PLUG DIDN'T run out to meet her as Charlie pulled up in the yard. She parked and looked around for the dog, wondering if he was over in the woods giving the squirrels a hard time.

She found the note on the kitchen counter. Her heart sank.

Emmett and I have taken Vera to the hospital. She's all right, so don't fret. She had a little fall. Her wrist might be broken. I didn't know where to find you. I'll call later, Selma.

Charlie fought tears. She should have been here. Now she had no idea what time they'd left. She picked up the phone and called Libby General Hospital and asked for the emergency room. It took only a few minutes before her aunt came on the line.

"Her wrist is broken," Selma said. "The doctor is going to put it in a cast and give her some medication to keep the pain down, but she's fine."

"I'll drive right up," Charlie said.

"No, there isn't any reason. Your mother is fine, really. But they've put her on pain pills and want to keep her overnight to see if there are any adverse reactions to the different drugs she's on. I was just getting ready to call you. I'm staying here with her."

"You're sure that's all there is to it?" Charlie asked. "I think I should be there."

"No. Your mother needs her rest and you would

just excite her. Bryan's here. He's going to take me out for a bite to eat.''

''The sheriff?''

''He heard Vera and I were in the hospital,'' Selma said. ''He told me about Wayne. I'm so sorry, Charlie.''

Charlie could do no more than nod at the phone. ''I'm not going to open the garage today.''

''Good. Make yourself a cup of tea and take a nice long hot bath,'' Selma said. ''That always helps.''

Charlie hung up, shaking her head. Her aunt thought a cup of tea could solve most any problem. But the hot bath did sound like a great idea.

The house seemed strange, alien to her, as if she hadn't spent the better part of the last twenty-six years here. As if she didn't know every creaking floorboard, every leaky faucet, every drafty corner.

It was the silence, she thought as she stopped in the living room. There'd seldom been silence in this house. Not with her mother and Selma chattering away as far back as Charlie could remember. There'd always been someone home when Charlie had returned from school, college, work. There'd always been something cooking on the stove and wonderful warm smells to come home to.

But standing in the large living room, the fireplace empty, only the soft tick of the old grandfather clock on the mantel, she got a sudden flash of the future without her mother, without her aunt, and the house felt as empty as she did. She couldn't bear it.

She moved through the house quickly, turning on lights and finally the water in the upstairs bathtub. She tried not to think. There was nothing she could do for Wayne. Her mother was fine. And Gus… The man was a fool, no wonder she couldn't get him out of her thoughts. She told herself he was doing this for a book. For his brother. Not her. No matter what he said.

Closing the bathroom door, she stripped off the overalls, the long underwear, the layers of clothing that she wore like a coat of armor to protect her from what? Men? Or from herself and a need to be held, to be loved and to love back?

As she stripped off the last layer of clothing, she realized there was only one man the armor hadn't protected her from. Gus.

Nothing could protect her from him because he'd seemed determined to tear down the wall she'd built around herself—even if it killed him, which she feared it would.

Where was he? Had he come to his senses and left town? The thought made her ache inside, and yet the thought of him staying here and getting hurt, possibly killed, devastated her.

She wondered how long it would be before Bryan came to arrest her. Maybe that's all the killer wanted, to see her behind bars. Gus would be safe.

The steam assaulted her as she stepped into the tub filled with hot water and closed the shower door after her.

As she slid down into the wonderfully warm water scented with bath beads and frothy with bubbles, she hoped to wash thoughts of Gus away—at least for a few moments. But the warmth of the water on her skin reminded her of his touch.

She felt the ache deep within her becoming unbearable. What had made her think she could live without the touch of a man? It had seemed possible before she'd met Gus. But now she knew that staying away from men wasn't the answer. Look what had happened to Josh. Someone had killed him and for what reason? Josh had never been interested in her romantically nor she him.

She turned on the hot water and let it run for a few minutes, steam rising until she felt wrapped in a cocoon of wet cotton. Leaning back, she closed her eyes, but not even the hot water could burn away thoughts of Gus from her mind, from her body. The memory of his kisses was imprinted on her lips just like the feel of being in his strong arms. For the first time in her life she was falling for someone. Her timing couldn't be worse. Nor her choice in men. Gus was all wrong for her. She sunk deeper in the hot water, trying hard not to cry.

A floorboard creaked downstairs in the living room. She opened her eyes, sitting up as she held her breath and listened. Another creak of the floorboards. Someone was downstairs.

THE PINECONE was fairly empty this early in the morning. T. J. Blue had taken a stool at the counter and was now hunched over his coffee cup.

"Good morning, Gus," Helen said. She slid a cup across the counter to him as he took a stool next to T.J. and thought about yesterday when he'd seen T.J. with Jenny Simonson.

T.J. didn't acknowledge his presence, but Gus could feel the tension coming off the man like a bad odor.

"Morning, Helen," Gus said, feeling as if he'd been in this town for weeks rather than days.

"The special's blueberry hotcakes, two eggs, side of ham and coffee. Three forty-nine."

"Just coffee," he said, not in the least hungry.

She filled his cup, remembering that he took it black, and moved off.

At the other end of the counter, Marcella was sitting on the second to last stool as usual, knitting. He wondered if the woman pretty much lived on that stool.

He overheard Helen tell Marcella that Trudi hadn't shown for work this morning.

"I saw you talking to Jenny Simonson yesterday," Gus said to T.J., figuring whatever was bothering the man would quickly become apparent.

T.J. swung his head around, his nostrils flaring, ready for a fight. "It's none of your business who I talk to."

"I couldn't help but notice that she seemed to have a black eye," Gus said quietly.

T.J. turned back to his coffee. "Also none of your business."

"Or yours?"

T.J. let out a snort. "You're just asking for it this morning," he said, keeping his voice down. The women were talking at the end of the counter. Gus didn't think they were paying any attention, but he figured Helen could probably listen to a half-dozen different conversations at once, given all her years in the diner.

"Didn't I hear that your car went off the road last

night?'' T.J. asked. "Take a hint. Somebody in this town doesn't like you."

"Any idea who that somebody might be?" Gus asked.

T.J. gave him a look that insinuated there were too many people to number and that T.J. himself was at the top of the list.

Gus took a sip of his coffee. "How long has Forest been knocking her around?"

T.J. didn't answer but tightened his grip on the coffee cup until his knuckles where white.

"You have to know what Forest will do when he finds out about the two of you," Gus said, wondering how far to push T.J. Wondering just how dangerous he might be.

The cup shattered in T.J.'s hand, coffee and pieces of white china skittering across the counter.

"What in the world?" Helen demanded as she hustled back down to them, a dishrag in her hand.

T.J. was on his feet. He threw a five-dollar bill onto the counter. "Sorry about the cup, Helen." With that, he turned and stalked out.

Helen eyed Gus. "Want to tell me what that was about?"

"Too much caffeine, I guess," Gus said, turning to watch T.J. leave, pickup tires spraying ice and snow. T.J. and Jenny. Gus swore, afraid what Forest would do when he found out. And how could he not in a town this size?

Helen sighed and gave Gus an impatient look. She cocked a hip against the counter as if settling in to give him a piece of her mind, but before the door could close behind T.J., it flew open. They both turned to see Trudi come in looking harried and apologetic.

She raced to the kitchen to dump her coat and purse, then came back and hurriedly filled Marcella's coffee cup.

Helen just groaned and looked away.

"More coffee?" Trudi asked, holding the pot over Gus's almost empty cup. She'd been cool toward him ever since that first night. Which was fine with him.

He shook his head. "Gotta go."

Emmett Graham came through the door as Gus was getting up to leave.

"Coffee, Emmett?" Helen said.

He nodded and slid onto a stool. "I just got back from Libby. Vera took a fall this morning. I ran her and Selma up to the hospital."

"Is Vera all right?" Gus asked, heart pounding.

Everyone looked at him for a moment before Emmett said, "Broke her wrist, but she's fine. They're keeping her overnight, a little concerned how the painkillers will react with the Alzheimer's medication. Selma's staying with her."

Gus felt a surge of relief, but it was short-lived. He glanced down the highway. Charlie was home alone.

"Is there a faster way to get to Charlie's than the county road?" he asked Emmett.

"There's a trail that cuts through the trees, but you'll have to cross the creek," he said as Gus rushed for the door. "You'll find it right across the way. Just take it north."

"Thanks," he called over his shoulder as he grabbed his coat and rushed out, unable to keep from thinking about his cut brake line, the person Spark Plug had chased away from the farmhouse last night, Charlie alone in that big old house. What if he was wrong about her being safe?

Chapter Sixteen

The first thing Gus saw was two sets of fresh tracks leading up the steps and onto the porch. Past the tracks, the front door stood ajar.

He hit the steps at a run. "Charlie? Charlie!"

From inside he heard a scream, followed by the sound of glass shattering. He didn't even think about grabbing a weapon on his way through the kitchen he was moving so fast. Nor did he realize he was screaming her name. "Charlie! Charlie!"

He heard the hammer of footfalls on the stairs and a door banging open. Then the haunting howl of a dog in the distance. Spark Plug? He rounded the corner of the living room in time to see movement through the pines on the side of the house.

Gus knew he'd never be able to catch the person— and he had to see to Charlie. He raced up the stairs.

"Charlie!" There were snowy wet prints on the stairs. He followed the prints to the partially opened bathroom door, scared to death of what he was going to find.

He stopped and slowly pushed open the door, his

heart in his throat. A sob came from inside the bathroom. "Charlie?"

"Gus!"

He rushed in to find the mirror over the sink shattered, shards of silver glittering on the tile floor. Charlie stood stark naked and dripping in the corner of the full tub, a bottle of shampoo clutched in her fist, half of the glass shower door gaping open, a look of pure terror on her face.

"Charlie," he said in a whisper and she leaped into his outstretched arms, dropping the shampoo to wrap her arms around his neck as he lifted her and carried her to the corner, away from the broken mirror. Grabbing a large, soft yellow towel from the rack, he pulled it around her, cradling her in his lap, in his arms. He held her to him as if that simple act could chase away all of their fears. "You're all right," he said against her wet hair, against the warmth of her cheek. "You're all right." He wasn't sure which one of them he was trying to convince.

After a few moments, he pulled back to look down into her face. The gold flecks in her brown eyes were electric, her color heightened by the heat of the shower and the fear. "You're all right," he whispered, desire making his voice hoarse and tight. "Can you stay here while I run downstairs and lock the doors?"

She nodded slowly.

When he returned just moments later with the robe he'd found in her bedroom, she was still huddled in the corner, the towel wrapped around her.

"I found Spark Plug closed up in the shed," he

said. "He's downstairs now and the doors are locked. You're safe."

"Thank you," she whispered.

"Did you see who it was?" he asked gently.

She shook her head. "All I saw was a dark figure through the steamy glass, then a gloved hand opening the shower door." She shuddered. "I guess I screamed, grabbed the conditioner bottle and threw it."

He nodded, kneeling down beside her. "It appears it hit the mirror." He touched her face, brushing away a tear with the rough pad of his thumb. "I called the sheriff, Charlie. He just picked up forest Simonson speeding on the county road about a half mile from here headed toward town."

"Forest." She looked up at him, tears welling in her eyes.

He reached for her, taking the towel as he slipped her into the robe.

Her fingers trembled as she tried to tie the sash. He took it from her. Her gaze came up to meet his. He tied the sash around her slim waist and brushed his fingertips across her cheek. Tears beaded on her lashes as she caught his fingers in her hand and brought them to her lips.

Her widened eyes locked with his, so filled with promise. He swept her up into his arms as if his whole life had been leading to this one moment in time.

She stretched up to kiss his cheek, then the corner of his mouth, then his lips, her breath warm and sweet. She pulled him down to her, her lips parting, clinging to him as if clinging to life. Her kiss a re-affirmation.

The need that had been smoldering between them for days burst into bright, flickering flame. She feathered light kisses across his face until her mouth lighted on his again, her taste sweet nectar. He wanted her like nothing he'd ever wanted before. He could feel the heat of her body, her skin hot against him even through all his clothing. He couldn't imagine his bare skin against hers. The thought made his knees weak.

Her fingers tugged at the buttons on his coat, burrowing under his shirt, her touch both pain and pleasure.

He carried her into her bedroom and set her on the bed. She pulled him down with her as her hands worked at his clothing. He brushed back a lock of her wet hair from her cheek with the pad of his thumb and cupped her jaw in his palm, drawing her face up, stilling her fingers.

"Charlie?" he said, his voice low and heavy with need.

She looked up into his eyes and slowly untied the sash of her robe. The fabric slipped from her slim shoulders. He watched her, desire molten inside him as he reveled in the body she'd kept hidden under all the clothing. How long had she been hiding that sexuality?

A lump rose in his throat, the ache in his chest making it hard to breathe. He didn't deserve this. Not after the way he'd treated her. "Charlie."

She touched her fingertips to his lips, her eyes lit with gold and unbridled desire. She smiled as she drew him closer. Her kiss was warm and demanding, her hands working again at his coat and shirt until she

had both off of him. A sigh escaped her lips as she
flattened her palms against his bare chest and looked
up at him. "Gus." It was all she said.

CHARLIE HAD NEVER KNOWN anything like it. She'd
had sex before, but she'd never been made love to.
Slowly, achingly, luxuriously made love to. The rest
of the day blurred with memories of his warm, strong
body, wrapped up in his arms in sleep and lovemaking. Whispered words, satisfied sighs and wonderful
restful sleep, free of fear as long as she was curled in
Gus's arms.

She woke, knowing before she even opened her
eyes that he was gone. Abruptly, she sat up, feeling
her heart lurch. Then she heard him downstairs and
smiled.

"Hello," she said from the kitchen doorway.

He turned and smiled, his gaze giving her a lazy
caress before he said, "I'm making hot chocolate and
sandwiches. I thought you might be hungry."

She returned his smile. "Not anymore."

"For food," he said quietly as he moved to her,
pulling her to him to give her a kiss.

"Actually hot chocolate and sandwiches sound
wonderful." She moved to the table where he had
one of the photo albums lying open.

"Just curious," he said to her inquiring look as he
placed two cups of cocoa and two plates with sandwiches on the table. "You were one cute little kid.
And one gorgeous woman," he said, nibbling at her
neck before he sat down next to her at the table.

This close to him, her skin felt as if touched by
flame. It was hard to breathe, hard not to just stare at

him, remembering everything they'd shared. She felt bowled over. By him. By the lovemaking. By this odd turn in her life. Gus had come here because of Josh's death. It gave her a strange feeling that also left her scared. For years she hadn't felt she deserved to be happy. Every time she tried, it was snatched away from her.

Only this time, she couldn't bear the thought. This time, it mattered too much.

"Is this you and Jenny?" Gus asked, changing the subject as he pointed to one of the photos.

She nodded as she looked at the photograph of the two of them. They must have been about six.

He flipped through a few more pages, stopping to smile at ones of her. "I thought I had a perfect childhood growing up on the ocean in Laguna Beach, but from the looks of these photos, yours was idyllic."

"It was," she had to admit. "Parents who doted on me, Aunt Selma..." She let out a sigh. "Actually a whole town, as small as Utopia is. People looked out for each other here."

"So it was good until Quinn died?" he asked.

She could feel him watching her closely. She nodded. That was when it had changed.

"Do we have to talk about this now? I mean, Bryan has Forest in custody—"

He brushed his fingers across her cheek. "Yeah, baby, we do. The sheriff couldn't hold Forest. All he could do was give him a speeding ticket. Bryan suggested you get a restraining order against Forest in the morning."

"That's it?"

"Afraid so, Charlie. There's no proof that Forest's

the one who was in the house earlier, you didn't get a good look at him and he was wearing gloves. Also he didn't do anything more than come into the house. The door wasn't locked. No breaking and entering. No assault.''

She sighed.

''Also, we can't be sure he's the one who's trying to frame you for Josh's murder,'' Gus said quietly. ''Forest is just the hothead among the suspects. I wouldn't rule out Phil Simonson or T. J. Blue at this point. Also Trudi Murphy seems to have an ax to grind. And there's Earlene, who was pregnant with his son. There were probably other women...''

She'd thought of that. ''You're wrong about Earlene.''

''I hope so. I like her.''

Charlie reached over to flip through the pages of the photo album, her thigh brushing his as she leaned toward him. She stopped at one large color photograph of what appeared to be senior prom.

''You looked beautiful,'' Gus said, ignoring the boy in the prom photograph to stare at Charlie in a formfitting emerald-green prom dress that accentuated everything about her.

''Thank you.'' She sounded shy, embarrassed.

He shifted his gaze to the man next to her in the photo and felt a jolt he couldn't explain. Was it just jealousy? ''There's something I don't understand. You and Quinn had broken up, right? So why did you even get in the car with him that night, let alone let him take you to the lake?''

She let out a short, harsh laugh. ''Let him? Quinn

did pretty much what he wanted. But I wouldn't have gotten into the car at all if it hadn't been for Jenny.''

Gus jerked back as if surprised. ''Jenny?'' He felt a sharp stab of recognition slice through him. Jenny and Quinn. Was it possible there was a reason her baby looked so much like Earlene's?

''Quinn had been flirting with Jenny, trying to make me jealous since our breakup. I was afraid he'd use her to get to me.''

''How did Jenny feel about Quinn?'' he asked, his heart pounding.

''I'm sure Jenny was flattered by the attention, but she was too smart to fall for it. Anyway, she must have been dating Forest.'' Charlie frowned. ''I'm sure she never told me about her and Forest because she knew I never liked him. I wanted to, when Jenny married him, but he made it impossible.''

''I've met Forest,'' Gus said. ''I would imagine he has always been an ass and that his bitterness over his brother's death has only made him worse.''

''I don't think Forest misses Quinn in the least. The two never got along. Forest was always horribly jealous of Quinn. Quinn was smart and popular and a good athlete and he was better-looking than Forest.'' She flipped back to a shot of Forest and Quinn when they were about five.

Gus felt his heart take off at a gallop. Skye Simonson and Arnie Kurtz couldn't have looked more like Quinn.

''Charlie.'' He pointed to the photograph. ''Are you sure Jenny wasn't interested in Quinn? You have to have noticed how much Skye and Arnie resemble each other—and Quinn.''

She stared at the photo of Quinn when he was about Skye's and Arnie's age. Tears welled in her eyes. "Oh, Gus, you don't think—"

"You said you weren't aware of her dating Forest," Gus said, ticking off the points. "Quinn was after Jenny to make you jealous. And given when Jenny and Earlene gave birth and how much their babies resemble Quinn…"

Charlie felt as if she'd been kicked by a mule. She leaned back, pushing the photo album away the same way she wanted to push away even the suggestion… "Oh, no," she whispered. Suddenly so many things made sense. Why she'd been so surprised when Jenny had married Forest. "I had no idea Jenny was even pregnant, but I wondered why she was in such a rush to marry Forest. Jenny said they'd been dating in secret. But why would they have done that?"

Jenny and Quinn. Of course. Charlie closed her eyes, the betrayal just as painful now as it would have been seven years ago. Hadn't she suspected Quinn was seeing someone else long before she'd heard about Earlene Kurtz's pregnancy?

She felt sick remembering. "If it's true—" She remembered how suddenly Jenny didn't call or stop by. The distance between them had started *before* Quinn's death, before Jenny's engagement and rushed marriage to Forest, before anyone suspected Charlie Larkin of murder.

She opened her eyes, brushed at the tears.

"I'm sorry," Gus said.

"It's not Quinn. I knew Quinn wasn't faithful, but I really didn't care. It's Jenny. She was my best friend. But if you're right, it explains a lot of things," Charlie said quietly.

"Like why Forest abuses her?" he asked.

She looked up, surprised. "Forest never seemed to care anything about Skye," she said, realizing it was true. "Or Jenny for that matter."

"I assume Jenny was at the party that night at the lake?".

She nodded, wondering where he was going with this.

"I was just thinking about two scared pregnant young women witnessing Quinn trying to get you back at the party and I can imagine how they must have felt," Gus said.

She stared at him for a moment, then got up and went to the window. "They must have hated Quinn. And me."

He came up behind her, his large hands touching her shoulders lightly. He began to rub away the tension knotted in her muscles. She let out a sigh and leaned into his strong hands, closing her eyes.

"You told Josh all of this," he said, working her shoulders, his hands heaven. "Did you mention names?"

She nodded.

"So he knew all the players," Gus said.

"What are you thinking?" she asked, not wanting him to stop what he was doing to her, not wanting to open her eyes.

"Josh tried to contact you—he had the locket Quinn had given you, the one you threw at Quinn the night of his death," Gus said. "It's a leap, but in order for him to have the locket in his possession, it is reasonable that he had some contact with whoever has had the locket all these years. Whoever picked it up at the party. That person must have given Josh the locket or left it where he could find it.''

Gus let go of her and moved back to the photo album. ''All of our suspects were at the party that night, right? Any one of them could have picked up the locket. But what connection could they have had with an emergency room doctor in Missoula?''

She had opened her eyes and was watching him.

''Miles found out that Phil Simonson was taken to the Missoula hospital the day of his logging accident,'' Gus said. ''Josh was on duty. That means Forest and Jenny were probably there. Earlene also took her son to the emergency room when Josh was on duty in another incident.''

''I see where you're going with this,'' she said. ''Josh might have gotten caught up in a single mother's life. Or an abused wife's.''

Gus nodded.

Charlie felt sick. ''There's something I need to tell you. I went back to the lodge last night after you left me at the lake. I'd noticed something on the floor by the fireplace. Someone has been hanging out up there. I found one of Quinn's toys on the floor. It was a toy that Arnie had taken from Skye Simonson at school and been forced to give back.'' She nodded, anticipating his next question. ''Skye got the toy back right before Josh's death.''

''Jenny,'' he said.

''I think she might go up there sometimes, maybe when Forest is being abusive,'' Charlie said, realizing what Gus suspected really could be true. No one had tried to help her. Except possibly Josh?

"I don't think she's been going up there alone," Gus said. "I saw her the other day with T. J. Blue behind the gravel pit off the main highway. She was in his arms."

Charlie stared at him, surprised. "T.J.? If Forest finds out—" Her heart dropped like a rock. "Oh, Gus, what if Forest suspected she was seeing someone and followed her to the lake. What if she was meeting Josh there?"

He swore. "This whole thing is starting to feel like a time bomb ready to go off and I'm afraid you're somehow at the center of it."

A cold chill stole up her spine. "You don't think Quinn's death was an accident, do you?"

"I don't know."

"I can't believe either Earlene or Jenny would do anything to hurt me," she said, praying that was true.

"What about Jenny's husband? Or father-in-law? Or Rickie Moss? If he thinks you're responsible for his scar..."

She covered her face with her hands. "I can't bear the thought that someone in this town hates me that much." She looked up at him, tears blurring her eyes. "These are people I've known all of my life. It is easier to believe it's some sort of curse or that—"

"That you might somehow be responsible?" he asked softly.

She nodded, tears stinging her eyes as they over-flowed.

He pulled her to him, wrapping his arms around her. "You aren't responsible. Don't worry, we'll find out who is. I promise you."

Chapter Seventeen

Charlie woke to darkness. She blinked and felt the side of the bed where she last remembered Gus's warm body. He was gone. Again. Then she heard the clatter of dishes and water running down in the kitchen. Hot chocolate and sandwiches again?

She glanced at the clock: 5:00 a.m. Pulling on her robe over her flushed nakedness, she hurried down the stairs, not wanting to spend even a moment out of his arms.

"Sleep well?" Helen asked with a knowing grin as she continued washing up the dishes in the sink.

"Where's Gus?" Charlie asked, noticing with disappointment that he was nowhere in sight—and his coat was missing from the hook by the back door.

"He had to take off for a while," she said with a shrug. "He asked me to hang out here until he got back. He told me about Forest—or at least that's who he thought got into the house." She shook her head. "Talk about a nutcase." She paused, eyeing Charlie. "You all right?"

Charlie nodded sheepishly and pulled her robe around her.

"It's nice to see a little color in your cheeks for a change," Helen said and smiled.

"Did he tell you where he was going?"

Helen shook her head. "Hungry? I could make you something."

"No, thanks." She shivered, wondering where Gus would take off to this time of the morning. It had to have been something important or he wouldn't have left her. That she was sure of. So what could have made him leave? "Who's opening the café this morning?"

"Trudi," Helen said and grimaced. "But Emmett promised to stop by and make sure she doesn't burn down the place." She laughed, then narrowed her eyes. "Don't try to run me off. I'm staying right here with you. No arguments."

Charlie saw that arguing would indeed be a waste of time. Her mind was on Gus and where he'd gone anyway. "I'll get some clothes on."

"I'll make us some coffee," Helen said.

As she started for the stairs, Charlie thought she remembered something from her sleep. The sound of the phone ringing. Just once. Gus must have answered it before it could ring again.

She hurried up the stairs, even more worried. She'd felt so safe in Gus's arms, but neither of them was safe, especially Gus. Especially now that they were lovers. If the killer found out—

The moment the caller ID came up she recognized the number. Her heart slammed against her chest. It was Jenny's old number, the one Charlie had called recently to ask her former friend to lunch. Jenny and

Forest's number. He'd called the house. Talked to Gus. And now Gus was gone. To meet Forest?

She dressed quickly in jeans and a sweater, unable to go back to wearing baggy clothing after a night with Gus, all the time, her mind racing. What could Forest have said that would convince Gus to go out at this hour?

Picking up the phone, she dialed the number, not sure what she planned to say when Jenny answered. All she could hope was that Jenny would know where Forest had gone.

"Hello."

Charlie was too startled to speak at first. "Forest?"

Silence, then, "What the hell do *you* want?" He sounded as if she'd awakened him. She didn't know what to say, afraid to ask for Jenny, afraid to ask why he'd called now that she was sure he wasn't with Gus.

She started to hang up when he swore, then demanded, "Where the hell is Jenny? Don't think I don't know that she's been meeting you behind my back." He let out a laugh that held no humor.

She could hear the rustle of clothing being hurriedly pulled on.

"She thinks I'm a fool, that I don't know where she goes and who she meets. She thinks I don't know about her little secret hiding place at the lake." It sounded as if he'd dropped the phone.

She could hear him banging around, then cursing something about "that cheating, lying bitch." But it was his last words before he hung up the phone that had her shaking. "I'm going to kill her. I'm going to kill them both."

Charlie stared at the phone for a heartbeat, then

dropped the receiver back into the cradle. If Forest hadn't called Gus to meet him, then Jenny had. She tore down the stairs.

Helen looked up, eyes wide as Charlie jerked the shotgun down from the top shelf and hurriedly dug a half-dozen shells from the kitchen drawer.

"Charlie?" Helen asked, sounding scared.

"Call Sheriff Olsen. Tell him that Gus has gone to the lake to meet Jenny. Forest is on his way up there, threatening to kill her. Kill them both." Charlie pulled her coat from the hook by the back door and shrugged into it. She picked up the shotgun. "I'm going up there to warn Gus."

"With a shotgun?" Helen asked.

"How long has Gus been gone?"

Helen glanced at the clock. "About fifteen minutes. But he said not to let you leave until he got back."

Charlie raised an eyebrow. "You aren't going to try to stop me, are you?"

Helen smiled sadly and shook her head. "I've known you far too long to know not to even try. I'll call Bryan right now." She reached for the phone. "Just be careful. Forest is more dangerous than anyone knows. I've been trying to tell that dumb Trudi that. I swear she's been moon-eyed over that idiot since high school."

Charlie headed for her VW van, putting everything out of her mind except Gus. She had to get to the lake before Forest. Either way, the sheriff wouldn't be far behind her. With luck she could reach Gus in time.

As she passed the large old tree outside her bedroom window, she was reminded of the summer she and Jenny were twelve. Charlie used to climb down the tree late at night to meet Jenny. They'd formed their own club and met in the barn. It was their little secret.

Jenny. Charlie couldn't help but wonder what other secrets Jenny might have been keeping all these years. The photos in the album haunted Charlie as she drove out to the county road. How could she not have seen how much Arnie and Skye looked alike and what that had to mean? How could she not have known about Jenny and Quinn?

Because she hadn't wanted to, she realized. She hadn't wanted to see, just as she hadn't wanted to see why Jenny had married Forest, why she'd put up with his abuse all these years.

Is that why Jenny had called the house? Because she needed help? Or did Jenny know who had murdered Josh? Is that what she'd lured Gus up to the lake with?

Josh had been the kind of man who would have also agreed to meet Jenny at the lake, Charlie thought with a chill. Josh knew about Jenny almost drowning there. He knew about the Simonsons' old lodge. Jenny might have even lost her virginity there to Quinn—just as Charlie and Earlene had. And if it was Jenny who'd been going up to the lake, hiding out in the lodge with Skye, to get away from Forest—

But how could Jenny find solace in that lodge given that Quinn had taken advantage of her there? Unless Jenny really had been in love with Quinn. Was it possible that Jenny had good memories of the lodge— and Quinn? That thought startled Charlie. If Jenny had been in love with Quinn then it also made sense that she could harbor ill feelings toward Charlie.

She drove down the highway, the sky still dark, the pines etched black against it. It hurt to even think about Jenny. Sometimes the truth stared her in the face and she refused to see it. Like Skye's uncanny resemblance to Quinn. Like the town ignoring Forest's abuse of Jenny. And Jenny taking it.

Charlie felt guilty for not doing something to help her friend. But what could she have done that wouldn't have made matters worse? Forest hated Charlie, blamed her for Quinn's death. As long as Charlie had stayed away from Jenny— With a jolt Charlie realized she hadn't done that. She'd asked Jenny to lunch and Forest had known. Had she put her friend in worse danger?

And now Forest was headed for the lake. Just as he had the night Josh Whitaker died?

In her headlights, Charlie saw the turnoff to Freeze Out Lake ahead and slowed, anxious to get there, to get to Gus to warn him about Forest. She had the shotgun on the seat next to her. The thought frightened her. But not as much as Forest hurting Gus.

She turned onto the narrow dark road, the tall pines closing in around the van as she started up the mountain. The van's headlights shone into the darkness, reminding her of the night Quinn had brought her up here, the night he'd died. She'd been so angry with him, demanding he take her back to town, but him ignoring her. Then at the party, when she'd found out about Earlene being pregnant with his baby—

She shifted down as the road switchbacked up the mountain, higher and higher as it carved a narrow path through the dense trees. It was almost six. It would be getting light soon.

The darkness reminded her again of the night Quinn died. Who'd been standing on the edge of her vision when she'd thrown the locket at Quinn? She'd been so angry with him, she hadn't paid any attention. But someone had picked up the locket. Quinn? No, the locket would have been found on his body after the wreck.

Suddenly her headlights picked up a vehicle in the road ahead. Gus's rental car was stopped in the middle of the road, blocking it. Another vehicle had tried to go around it, but had gotten stuck in the trees.

She stopped as she recognized Forest's truck, snow up to the wheel wells. Oh God, he was ahead of her. In the light of her headlamps, she could see from where she was that the cabs of both vehicles were empty. There were tracks in the snow near the pickup where Forest had taken off on foot up the mountain toward the lake.

There were several old logging roads that would get her to the lake, but she didn't want to take the time to backtrack. She pulled the van to the edge of the road behind Gus's rental car, careful not to get into the snow and get stuck like Forest had.

She could see now what had kept Gus from going any farther up the road. A large tree had fallen over. No, not fallen over, she thought as she stared out the windshield. She could see wood chips next to the base of the pine. Someone had cut down the tree—purposely blocking the road.

With trembling fingers, she hurriedly loaded the shotgun and put the rest of the shells in her coat pocket, then with her flashlight in hand, she climbed out of the van and started up the mountain.

The snow had melted back from the road, the cold night had made the ground hard. She'd left no tracks.

She hadn't gone far up the road when she spotted tracks cutting through the snow and trees on what appeared to be a path. Forest's tracks. Did he know a shortcut to the lodge?

She followed his tracks, praying she would reach the lodge in time.

As she walked, she forced herself to remember the night of Quinn's death. The locket. She tried to see herself throwing it at him, turning… She could recall images off to the side. Forest was there by his brother. T.J. off by the campfire. Earlene had gone to one of the cars, upset and crying. And Jenny—

Suddenly Charlie had a flash of memory so sharp it almost blinded her. She stumbled. Jenny had been standing beside her that night. As Charlie had turned away, she'd seen Jenny stoop down to pick up the locket from the dirt!

DARKNESS HAD DROPPED over the lake like a sack, clouds obscuring any stars or moon. But Gus knew daylight wasn't far off. He could make out the roof-line on the lodge to the east of him as the sky began to lighten.

He sat on a large rock by the shore, the lodge nearby, waiting, wondering if his brother had waited in this same spot. Only Josh hadn't known he was waiting for a killer. Gus knew it was more than a good possibility.

When Jenny had called, she'd been crying. She'd

wanted to talk to Charlie. Gus had calmed her down, offered to help. She'd said Forest was in the other room asleep, that he would kill her if he knew she had called Charlie, that she needed to get out of the house. She was going to the lake lodge. No, Skye was at a friend's house. Forest had been drinking and Jenny had wanted Skye out of the house.

She'd said she needed to tell someone the truth.

He'd agreed to meet her at the lake, knowing all the time that it was more than likely a trap.

He'd opted to wait out here in the open rather than in the lodge. When he'd found the tree across the road and realized it had been sawed down, he hadn't been surprised. Just a little more anxious. He was finally going to find out who'd killed his brother. Who was trying to frame Charlie.

On the way up the mountain, walking through the dark of the pines, he'd asked himself why he was doing this. Risking his life. It had started out as vengeance and repentance, finding Josh's killer, writing a book that would vindicate Augustus T. Riley of any guilt about his brother.

Then he'd met Charlie, fallen for her like a rock from a cliff. Now more than ever he wanted the killer. He never wanted to see fear on Charlie's face again—not like he'd seen last night.

He also wanted to make up for all those years he hadn't been close to Josh. Had resented his younger half brother.

He felt no small amount of guilt for being angry at his mother when she'd remarried so soon after his father's death. Then when she'd become pregnant right away with Josh—

Gus shook his head, thinking of all the years he'd wasted by being angry. Feeling left out. Not that it helped that Josh had been nothing short of a saint. So different from Gus.

He shook off the memories, letting his flashlight beam skitter across the road ahead of him. In the distance, he could smell the lake. Where was Jenny? Or had she never planned to come? Had she always planned to send Forest instead?

He ached to flick on the flashlight, even for an instant, and chase away the darkness. It closed in on him, so thick it seemed to have texture and substance. Just like the silence.

Then he heard it. The sound of a vehicle grew louder and louder, the rusted-out muffler making a throbbing sound that echoed through the trees. The same pickup he'd heard last night when his brake line was cut?

The truck stopped in the pines, the engine dying, pitching the lake back into that awful eerie silence.

Gus listened to the pickup's door creaking open, then clicking closed. He held his breath, his gun ready.

A flashlight beam cut through the pines toward the lodge. Whoever it was had known about another road to the lake.

Gus pushed himself up off the rock and headed toward the bobbing light, hanging back just enough he hoped he wouldn't be heard. The person with the flashlight headed for the lodge, straight as an arrow. Was it Jenny?

He thought he heard what sounded like another vehicle coming up the lake road as he walked, but when he stopped he heard only silence. He was almost to the lodge when a limb cracked like a gunshot somewhere behind him, making him jump. Closer, he heard the door to the lodge groan open.

He could see nothing in the darkness of the trees behind the lodge.

Through the broken slats of the shutters, a flashlight beamed flickered. If it was Jenny, wouldn't she call out for him?

Gus moved closer to the lodge, stumbling in the dark, but determined not to use his flashlight, not to give away his position. Another limb cracked off to his right, behind the lodge. He stopped to listen again, suddenly afraid there was more than one person out there. Worse, one was tracking the other.

He hoped to hell it was just some small rodent— and not a grizzly looking for a quick meal before hibernation.

Someone was moving around inside the lodge as if looking for something. The toy that Charlie had found? What other evidence could there be?

Cautiously, Gus moved closer, wondering if he dared climb the creaky steps to the porch or if he should wait until his visitor came back out to confront whoever it was.

Forest's angry voice suddenly shattered the quiet night. "What the hell are *you* doing here?" Forest demanded. "What the hell—" Gus heard what sounded like scuffling. He rushed the steps, but as he reached the porch, from inside came the thump of something heavy hitting the floorboards. He edged toward the door, half expecting someone to come flying out any moment.

Silence. The occasional creak of a floorboard. The screech of an owl on the other side of the lake. Then that awful silence again.

He cautiously pushed open the door and, with the weapon in one hand and the flashlight in the other, he burst in, shining the light ahead of him into the room.

Forest Simonson was sprawled in a pool of blood on the floor in front of the fireplace. Gus swept the light around the room, his hand shaking. The room was empty. The attacker apparently gone.

Gus quickly knelt beside Forest, putting down the flashlight as he felt for a pulse. Blood gurgled up through a cut in Forest's coat at heart level. Forest struggled to speak, his lips moving, but nothing coming out. His fingers clutched at Gus's coat sleeve, pulling him closer.

As Gus bent over him, he caught Forest's whispered last word. "Jenny." Then the fingers gripping his coat sleeve released and Forest Simonson was gone.

Gus got to his feet, the hair on the back of his neck standing on end, the cold room suddenly short of oxygen. He shone the flashlight around the lodge again. Whoever had stabbed Forest had escaped.

But Gus didn't think the killer had left the lake. Just the lodge.

He turned off the flashlight and stood in the pitch blackness listening, expecting someone to jump him at any moment and bury the blade in his chest before he could get off a shot. Thank God Charlie was safe back at the house.

Hurriedly, he turned on his flashlight again. The

beam fell on drops of blood a few feet from Forest's body on the dusty floor along with two sets of footprints. He followed the bloody trail and the tracks to a back entrance to the lodge. The door stood open. There was blood on the steps and drops on the dried pine needles at the head of what appeared to be a trail.

THE GROUND LEVELED OFF some and Charlie knew she had to be nearing the lodge. She scrambled through the pines along the narrow game trail, climbing over downed trees and around boulders, following the thin insignificant beam of the flashlight up the mountain, the shotgun cumbersome.

The darkness in the pines felt so close it was suffocating. At times, she stopped to listen, imagining that she was being followed. But those times, she could hear nothing over the pounding of her heart. Even if she hadn't been half running to reach Gus, her heart would have hammered with the fear and worry she felt. She had to get to him before the killer did. She had to warn him.

The trail swung off to the right. She knew she was close now. She and Jenny had spent many summers up here at the lake with their parents before that incident in high school, the almost drowning. Charlie had forgotten all the good times with Jenny. Now they came back in a rush and she felt sick with worry that she knew who the killer was.

She came around a large pine that encroached on the trail and for an instant thought she'd conjured up the image standing in the middle of the trail.

She stumbled to a stop, heart in her throat as the penlight beam illuminated Jenny's face.

"Charlie." Jenny's eyes seemed too bright, reminding Charlie of Wayne's when he was excited or upset. Jenny stood, one arm at her side, the other slightly behind her as if she was holding her side. She looked out of breath and Charlie realized that Jenny could have been running to get ahead of her and cut her off.

"Jenny, what are you doing here?" The words came out on a hoarse breath.

"I'm sorry," Jenny whispered and rubbed her lips with her visible hand as if agitated. She wore no gloves and in the light Charlie could see that her hand was bright red from the cold. "I never meant to hurt anyone."

Charlie's heart leaped to her throat. *Be cool.* "Who did you hurt, Jenny?" she asked softly.

Jenny looked dazed as she met Charlie's gaze. "Quinn."

"Quinn?" Charlie thought she must have heard wrong.

"I went after him that night, you know, on this trail until it came to the road. He stopped when he saw me standing in the middle of the road, waiting for him. He smiled and opened the door for me as if he'd known I'd come after him. As if it was always me he wanted. Not you."

Charlie felt her blood run cold. She'd forgotten about the shotgun, heavy in her left hand, and realized she would have to drop the flashlight to fire the weapon. The thought skittered past. She could never shoot Jenny and she knew it. Is that why Jenny hadn't even seemed to notice the shotgun Charlie carried? Jenny stood not six feet from her. On either side there was nothing but dense trees and underbrush. If Charlie made a run for it, she would have to just bust through the pines and hope for the best.

"He put his arm around me while he drove." Jenny smiled, as if lost in the past, but tears spilled down her cheeks and she never took her eyes off Charlie as she talked. "I was so sure everything was going to be all right. I told him about the baby we made that night at the lodge. I thought he'd forgive me for lying about being on the Pill. I loved him so much, I knew I could make him happy. Happier than you ever could."

"Oh, Jenny, I never knew," Charlie whispered, seeing the pain in her once–best friend's face.

"You never knew because you were so busy playing hard to get with Quinn," Jenny snapped. "It's the only reason he kept chasing you."

Charlie felt a chill as she realized the depth of Jenny's pain and anger.

Jenny's demeanor instantly changed. She cocked her head to one side as if she was listening to someone Charlie couldn't see. "Quinn said horrible things to me," Jenny said in a childlike voice. "Horrible things. I started hitting him, trying to make him stop. He was yelling at me and driving so fast. He hit me hard. Knocked me across the seat. I felt the car swerve and crash." Jenny's eyes were wide, dazed, her voice rising, her words coming faster. "I must have blacked out. Quinn was dead. I crawled out the car window. I walked back up the road to the party. No one even missed me."

"It wasn't your fault," Charlie tried to reassure her. "It was an accident."

"That's what Josh said and now he's dead, too," Jenny snapped.

Josh. Oh God, Josh. Charlie felt the air rush from her lungs as if Jenny had hit her. She began to shake, her teeth rattling from the cold, the horror. *Dead, too?* Who else was dead? Not Gus. Oh, please God, not Gus.

"Where is Gus?" Charlie asked, her voice cracking.

Jenny didn't seem to hear. "Josh thought I was staying with Forest as penance for what I'd done. He thought he could help me." Jenny leveled her gaze at Charlie. "He wanted me to tell you about Quinn. To free you from the curse of Quinn's death and free myself from Forest." She let out a harsh laugh. "Like Forest would ever let me be free. Once he found your locket in Quinn's car—" She glared at Charlie as if it had all been her fault. "Forest saw me pick it up from the ground where you'd thrown it. He knew."

Charlie stared at her, shocked. "Forest *blackmailed* you into marrying him?" Forest had used his brother's death to get Jenny and then abuse her, knowing she could never leave him with Quinn's death hanging over her head. And he'd blamed Charlie all this time when he'd *known* she hadn't killed his brother. She felt sick. If only Jenny had told the truth years ago.

"I begged Josh not to come up here," Jenny was saying. She was crying now. "Josh thought he could talk some sense into Forest, *reason* with him. He thought *talking* was the answer. Him and his stupid help lines. I should never have called. I should never have told him about Quinn, about Forest.''

Over Jenny's crying, Charlie heard a car coming up the lake road. Sheriff Bryan Olsen.

"Listen, Jenny, I'm freezing. Let's walk on down to the lodge—'' She had to find Gus.

"We can't go down there,'' Jenny said as she swiped at her tears with her free hand and slowly withdrew her other hand out from behind her.

The blade of the knife she had gripped in her fingers caught in the beam of Charlie's flashlight. Even from where she stood, Charlie could see the blood on the long slender filet blade. Her heart lunged. No!

"It's not safe down there,'' Jenny said, holding up the knife. "Ask Forest.''

Charlie moved without thinking, without feeling. She dived into the pines off to her left, the boughs gouging at her face and clothing as she ran blindly in the direction of the road—and the lodge, the flashlight beam bobbing wildly as she ran. She thought she could hear Jenny behind her, almost feel the sharp blade cut through her coat as she barreled through the trees, jumping over fallen logs and off boulders. At some point, she threw the heavy, cumbersome shotgun off into a small ravine, thick with timber, and kept running.

She fell once and scrambled to her feet, but didn't look back for fear she would see Jenny. Not the Jenny who'd once been her best friend, but someone else in Jenny's body. Jenny had traded the truth and her freedom for her own private hell and now Charlie was at the center of it. Maybe always had been.

Through a break in the pines, Charlie spotted the road ahead. Just a few more yards.

She could hear a car, knew it had to be the patrol car. He must have come up one of the old logging roads. The sheriff would have a gun and could use it. Together they would find Gus. Everything was going to be all right now. She knew who the killer was.

Suddenly Charlie was jerked off her feet. A hand clamped down over her mouth before she could get a scream out and she was dragged back into the trees, struggling with her last breath. The flashlight fell from her fingers and then there was only darkness.

"Charlie, it's me—Gus. I've got you, baby. It's okay."

She closed her eyes and let the tears come as he released her and she turned to let him take her, never having been so happy in her life as to be in his arms again.

"Oh, Gus, it's Jenny," she cried against his shoulder.

"I know, I heard everything," he said, holding her as if he'd never let her go.

"Gus, I'm scared. She had a knife. It had blood on it."

"I know, baby. Forest is dead in the lodge. He was stabbed," Gus whispered back. "We have to get out of here."

Chapter Eighteen

Gus had followed the blood trail from the old lodge until the drops became fewer and fewer and finally ran out. The pines were dense and dark and he had started to turn back when he'd heard Charlie's voice. He'd started to call to her, but then he'd heard Jenny's strained words and had frozen in midstep. He'd listened to Jenny's confession and decided the only reason she was telling Charlie was that she didn't plan to let Charlie live long enough to tell anyone. Forest was already dead.

But he didn't dare try to get closer and he couldn't see Jenny from where he stood to get off a shot. He knew he couldn't get to Jenny before she got to Charlie. It was too dangerous to try. He also knew Charlie couldn't use the shotgun—not against Jenny. So he'd waited, praying Charlie would apply that smart mind of hers. And she had. She'd taken off and he'd come after her.

"Do you hear that?" he asked next to her ear as the sound of a vehicle grew louder and louder until it was almost to them.

"It's the sheriff. I had Helen call him to follow me."

Gus didn't even want to know how she'd gotten away from Helen. Nor was it a good time to lecture her, although he certainly wanted to. He was still shaking at how close she'd come to getting herself killed.

The lights of the car flickered in the trees as the vehicle drove slowly down to the edge of the lake near the lodge and stopped.

"How did he and Forest get up the road?" Gus whispered to Charlie. "It was blocked when I came up."

"There are some old logging roads, if you know where to find them."

"I assume you chucked the shotgun?" he asked, afraid Jenny might now have it.

"I threw it down a ravine," she admitted sheepishly. "I couldn't use it, Gus. And it was too heavy to carry and run…"

"It's okay, baby," he said and pulled her closer.

Gus hadn't heard anything in the woods behind him but he couldn't be sure that Jenny wasn't out there, waiting to jump them. He didn't like staying in one place long. It felt safer to keep moving. And once they reached the sheriff—

He picked up Charlie's flashlight from the dried pine needles, turned it back on and handed it to her. He could see the road from where they stood. But if they stayed in the pines they could reach the car without exposing themselves to the open road. "Let's go."

They moved through the pines, edging closer to the

lake and the car. Off to his right, Gus could see the
lodge roof against the lightening sky. The lake shimmering in the gray light of the coming dawn beyond
the lodge.

As they drew closer to the vehicle, Gus hoped to
hell it *was* the sheriff. He doubted Jenny had driven
here with Forest, so she had to have her own vehicle.

In a break in the trees, Gus saw something that
made him stop. Charlie'd been right. It was Bryan's
patrol car. The engine was running, the headlights
shining out across the silver waters of the lake, the
driver's-side door open, the interior light glowing. But
there was no one behind the wheel.

Gus crouched down, pulling Charlie with him. He
motioned for her to be quiet. Had Bryan gotten out?
They waited for several long minutes, but there was
no sound of someone moving around. It was still too
dark to see in the pines.

Gus edged toward the patrol car with Charlie right
behind him. As soon as he reached the side of the
patrol car, he saw Sheriff Bryan Olsen sprawled
across the seat.

"No," Charlie whispered as Gus moved to the cop
and felt for a pulse.

"He's alive," Gus said. He turned off the headlights, but left the car running as he moved Bryan so
the door would close. The interior light went off. Gray
darkness fell over them like a thick blanket. The air
was cold and damp.

Charlie crouched and stayed against the side of the
patrol car, the shock starting to set in. Jenny. Tears
burned her eyes again, but she refused to break down

now. She swallowed back the pain, searching for the anger that would keep her strong.

Good ol' trusting Bryan. He would have opened his door to Jenny. Just as Josh must have. And Jenny was still out there.

"We need to get him to a doctor," Gus whispered. "Come around to the other side of the car with me. Once we're both in, lock the doors. We're going to take the patrol car and get out of here."

"Take me with you," said a voice out of the darkness.

Gus swung around, snapping on the flashlight, the gun in his other hand, as he moved to protect Charlie. The flashlight beam lighted on a dark figure just a few feet away in the pines.

"T.J.," Gus said, instantly on guard.

"Where's Jenny?" T.J. asked, glancing from the gun to Gus's face. He sounded scared.

"I don't know," Gus admitted.

"She'd dangerous," T.J. said. "Who knows what she'll do next."

"Did she ride up with you?" Gus guessed.

T.J. nodded and stepped a little closer, watching the gun in Gus's hand. He had both hands in his pockets, shoulders hunched as if he was cold. "She said she was worried about Forest. She talked me into following him up here. She was acting strange, saying she wasn't going to put up with his abuse anymore. When we got here, she jumped out of my truck and took off through the trees." T.J. glanced around behind him as if he feared she'd be coming after him next. "She had a knife."

"Forest is dead," Gus said. "He was stabbed."

"Oh, man," T.J. moaned, looking away. "I had no idea she was really going to hurt anyone." He met Gus's gaze. "I don't expect you to believe this, but I've been trying to help Jenny, that's all. She wanted to leave Forest, but she was afraid he'd kill her if she tried. He was mean to her, man."

A limb cracked in the pines nearby. Suddenly it seemed colder, as if an icy breeze had sneaked up off the lake. The sheriff groaned inside the patrol car.

"Where's your truck?" Gus asked.

"Back up the road," T.J. said. "She cut both my front tires."

Had Jenny planned to kill them all? Maybe she felt she had nothing to lose. A limb cracked, closer this time.

"We have to get the sheriff to a doctor," Gus said. They were all exposed standing out here with the flashlight on. Jenny could come out of the dark from any direction and kill one of them before they could react. "We'd better get going."

T.J. nodded and started toward them.

"Noooooooooo!" It came out of the forest, echoed across the lake, chilling Gus's blood.

Gus turned at the sound of Jenny's cry to open the patrol car door to get Charlie inside. T.J. hit him upside the head with something hard. Gus's legs buckled under him and he fell to his knees, dropping the flashlight. T.J. jerked the gun from his hand before Gus could get off a shot, slammed him against the side of the patrol car, shoving him down with a boot to his back—the icy barrel of the gun jabbing him in the back of the neck as stars glittered in his head and he fought not to pass out. He lay still, pretending he was out cold, waiting for the blackness to pass, waiting to make his move.

The flashlight had fallen to the cold ground, the beam shining toward the lodge, but Charlie could see T.J.'s face and the grin on it.

"You and your boyfriend think you're so damn smart," T.J. spat. He grabbed her arm and jerked her to him, encircling her neck with his arm in a headlock as he turned to face the pines and the lodge. "Come on out, Jenny, or I'll kill her!" he yelled. "You said you wanted to be free of Forest. Well, you're free. Thanks to me. So come on down here, Jenny. Don't I always take care of you? I'm going to take care of this, too. Just like I took care of that nosy doctor from Missoula. I'm the only one you can trust, Jenny."

Charlie let out a cry as T.J. tightened his hold on her. He still had the barrel of the gun pointed at Gus's back. "Pick up the flashlight," he ordered Charlie, forcing her to bend down with him.

She did as she was told, feeling light-headed. He was holding her so tightly around the neck, he was cutting off her oxygen.

"Shine it out in the trees," T.J. ordered. "No, over to the right by the lodge." The sky behind the trees had lightened to silver, making the darkness in the pines seem blacker.

She tried to pry his arm away with her free hand, but he only clamped down harder.

She had to do something and quick. She'd thought Gus was knocked out, but she saw him move his fingers like a signal. With the flashlight in her hand, she brought it down as hard as she could, connecting with

T.J.'s knee. A loud crack filled the air, then T.J.'s furious curse.

He shoved her away as he grabbed for his knee. Charlie stumbled and fell, losing the flashlight. It hit the shore and tumbled into the water. Fighting for air, she groped on the ground for the next best thing: a rock.

She turned to see T.J. trying to get into the patrol car, but Gus's body was in the way.

She rushed T.J., hitting him in the back of the head with the rock clutched in her hand at the same moment Gus grabbed T.J.'s injured leg. T.J. slammed into the patrol car as Gus scrambled to his feet.

T.J. let out a howl and grabbed a handful of Charlie's hair, putting her between him and Gus. "You stupid bitch." He shoved the barrel of the gun against her temple. "Make another move and I kill her!" he yelled at Gus.

Gus froze.

All Charlie caught at first was movement, something dark coming out of the misty blackness of the pines near the edge of the lake. Jenny rushed in, the knife in her hand, her eyes looking glazed in the new light of day, her teeth bared in a grimace as she buried the knife blade in T.J.'s back.

He screamed, releasing his grip on Charlie's hair. Jenny stumbled back drawing the knife out as T.J. spun around, the gun still in his hand.

Gus dived for him, taking T.J. down, but not before he got off a shot. The report echoed across the lake, loud as a cannon. Gus wrestled the gun away from T.J.

Charlie watched Jenny, afraid of what she'd do

next. But she stood, the knife in her hand still, her head cocked to one side, as if listening to a voice only she could hear. Then her gaze went to the lake where just a few feet offshore, the flashlight had landed, its beam now slicing through dark, gloomy waters like an elusive sea monster.

Jenny suddenly sat down hard on the rocky shore. Charlie reached for her and stopped when Jenny turned to look at her. The front of her coat was dark with blood where T.J. had shot her.

"I'm sorry," Jenny whispered, then looked past Charlie down the shore toward the old lake lodge. She smiled, looking young again. Her last word was "Quinn."

Epilogue

Charlie remembered little of the drive to Libby to the hospital—except for her last glimpse of the lake. The sun had climbed up, golden over the pines, setting the surface afire with color. Mist rose ghostlike from the water as the silken pines shimmered along the shore.

She had stared at it as Gus turned the patrol car around, wondering at how peaceful it looked, how beautiful—as if nothing horrible had happened here. Or ever would again.

Gus drew her close as they left. She didn't look back. She snuggled against him, but not even the warmth of his body could chase away the cold inside her.

At the hospital, she knew long before the doctor came out to tell them that Bryan had a concussion but would pull through, that Gus was leaving. She'd seen it in his eyes, felt it in the way he held her.

"I have to write this book," he said, his hands cupping her shoulders as his gaze held hers. "I need to do this for myself, for my brother."

She nodded, understanding what he was saying. He

couldn't do it without leaving her. Hadn't she known that from the first?

"I do understand," she said and smiled as she reached up to brush the tips of her fingers across his stubbled jawline.

He closed his eyes as if in pain. "Charlie, what happened between us—"

She silenced him, pressing her fingers to his lips.

He opened his eyes and pulled her into his arms, hugging her hard and long, her face pressed against his chest.

She listened to the beat of his heart, a sound she knew she would never forget.

The days that followed were little more than a painful blur. Jenny and Forest were buried in the small cemetery outside town. Jenny's parents didn't come back from Florida to attend. But the rest of the town was there as they hadn't been for Jenny during her life.

Forest was buried next to his brother, Quinn. Phil broke down over his sons' graves, alone as he'd never been before.

Gus stayed for the burials, then left. "I won't be calling for a while," he said. "I can't, not if I hope to get this story down."

She'd kissed him, her mother and aunt gazing from the kitchen window, and stood watching him drive away from the farmhouse until the rental car disappeared in the pines.

She threw herself back into her work, taking on Leroy's old snowplowing tractor even though she knew she couldn't get parts for it. So she made the parts she needed, determined to get it running as if making that ancient tractor run were a matter of life and death.

Earlene filed papers to adopt Jenny and Forest's little girl, Skye. Phil Simonson didn't even put up a fight. In fact, he started going over to spend time with his two grandchildren on Sunday afternoons. Earlene said the first time he held Arnie and Skye in his arms, Phil wept like a baby.

T.J. was in jail, denied bail, awaiting trial. From his cell, he told a classic tale of love and betrayal, sex and seduction, jealousy and murder that was repeated over the lunch special at the Pinecone, until it had taken on a life of its own.

To the end, T.J. saw himself as Jenny's hero. He'd tried to save her from Forest, a man who'd blackmailed Jenny into marrying him but soon realized that while he might be able to keep Jenny with the horrible truth he held over her, he couldn't make her love him. When Skye looked so much like his brother, Forest became even more bitter and had began to take it out on Jenny.

But T.J. had demanded almost as much as Forest had of Jenny. He would keep her secrets, but she must always turn to him. Jenny made the mistake of calling the help line one night and pouring out her soul to Josh Whitaker. Later she would meet Josh at the hospital when her father-in-law was injured in the logging accident. Josh would have recognized Jenny as an abused woman.

T.J. had found out about Josh's plan to meet Jenny at Freeze Out Lake and get her to tell the truth about Quinn and free herself from Forest—and free Charlie as well.

T.J. had gotten there first, killed Josh and disposed of the body and car, believing he was protecting Jenny. Jenny had thought Forest had killed Josh and taken on that guilt as well until it had become a tangled web of lies.

Bryan was released from the hospital after a few days. Selma insisted he come stay at the farmhouse until he had completely recuperated. By the end of the week, Bryan had retired as sheriff and asked Selma to marry him to everyone's surprise. Finally, Charlie understood the never-worn wedding dress in the attic. Bryan had been her mystery beau all those years ago. Selma turned Bryan down, just as she had all those years ago, saying she had to take care of her sister. Bryan said he would wait for her. Just as he always had.

The day before Thanksgiving, Charlie was in the garage. She'd been working on Leroy's old tractor and had just started it up, more than pleased when it finally ran.

She was hoping it was an omen of good things to come, when she looked up to see Gus standing in the gas station office doorway.

At first she thought he was only a mirage, she'd imagined him standing there so many times. But then he walked toward her and she caught the scent of his aftershave.

She wiped her hands on a rag, watching him, wondering what he was doing here, her heart pumping so hard it hurt.

"Leroy's tractor?" Gus asked, glancing past her to the monstrous orange machine behind her.

She could do no more than nod as he closed the

distance between them. The moment he touched her, her heart began to pound even harder. He was flesh and blood. No mirage.

He traced a finger along her lips, then down the slim column of her throat to the hollow between her breasts, his gaze locked with hers.

"God, I've missed you," he whispered. He pulled her to him and dropped his mouth to hers with a hunger than made her stagger. His kiss brought it all back, the wonder of their lovemaking, the pain of his leaving.

She pulled back, shaking inside with need for him—and a fear that unlike the first time he walked in here, this time he really was just passing through. "What are you doing here?"

"Isn't it obvious?" he asked as he dropped to one knee on the cold concrete. "I'm asking you to marry me."

Her heart lodged in her throat, tears springing to her eyes. She was shaking her head, unable to find words, her disappointment was so great.

She couldn't possibly marry him. Didn't he realize that she couldn't leave Utopia? Couldn't leave her mother and aunt? Or the garage? Not even for him.

"Don't turn me down until you hear the proposal," he said, nonplussed. "I want to marry you, Charlie, but you have to know first that you'd be marrying an unemployed dreamer who has always dreamed of writing the great American novel in some small, out-of-the-way town in Montana."

She stared at him. "Since when?"

"Since I met you." He smiled, his eyes bright with love.

"Are you sure?" she had to ask.

He nodded. "When I finished the book about my brother and his death, I knew I was finished with that part of my life. I don't want to write about murder or the lives it devastates anymore, Charlie. I can't. It's not in me anymore, not since you."

He pulled a small velvet box from his pocket and held it out to her. "Say you'll marry me. You wouldn't want to destroy a man's dream, would you?"

She took the velvet box in her trembling fingers and opened it. A beautiful diamond ring winked up at her. "You really think you can live here and be happy?"

"What man wouldn't want to live in Utopia," he joked, then said, "Honey, this floor is very cold and hard. I'd live with you anywhere. I've never been more sure of anything in my life. Say yes so I can get up."

"Yes!" She threw herself into his arms as he straightened.

He kissed her slowly as if savoring the taste of her, then he drew back to take the ring from her and put it on her finger.

"You realize we will be living in the farmhouse with my aunt and mother," Charlie warned.

"I already talked to Selma," Gus said. "She says once we get the nursery added on there will be plenty of room for all of us. Emmett said he'd start working on it right away."

"Nursery?" Charlie asked.

He cupped her face in his hands. "When were you planning to tell *me?*"

"What?"

"About the baby," Gus said.

"What baby?"

"The one Selma says you're going to have." Gus grinned at her. "Don't worry, she didn't tell me until after I'd told her about the ring—and my plans. I assured her that I've saved enough money to support you until I sell my first work of fiction. I also have royalties coming in from the crime books, but that's not the kind of legacy I want to leave to our children."

"I'm going to have a baby?" Charlie asked, still in shock. She knew it was way too early to know if their lovemaking had made a baby.

"Just in time for the Fourth of July celebration here in Utopia, according to your aunt."

Charlie began to laugh. Her aunt the seer.

Gus swung her up into his arms. She caught a glimpse of the future in his eyes and could see their stories woven into the fabric of the town. Gus and Charlie and their children.

As Gus put her down, Charlie looked over by the workbench, wishing her father could have been here. He was standing in his spot, his coffee cup in his hand. He glanced at Leroy's tractor and gave her a thumbs-up. Then he looked at Gus and nodded his approval. Slowly he put down his coffee cup. She felt tears rush her eyes as her father started for the door. She heard his words in her head as he stopped and turned, "You're going to be just fine now." Then he was gone.

"Are you all right?" Gus asked, thumbing away

the tears on her cheeks as he looked down into her face, worry in his eyes.

She nodded. "I'm going to be just fine now."

Gus kissed her again, then worked the top button of her shirt free.

She let out a sharp intake of breath as he freed the next button, then another one, his fingers brushing her warm skin.

"I couldn't bear to spend another day away from you," he said as he slipped a strap of her overalls off her shoulder. "I've been thinking about getting you out of these clothes for the last hundred miles." He slid the other strap from her shoulder. The baggy overalls dropped to the floor.

"What if someone comes by for gas?" she protested as he continued to undress her.

"There's a can out on the pump. They can just help themselves and leave the money." He grinned. "I also locked the front door and put up the Closed sign on my way in."

"How did you know I'd be here?"

"I know *you,* Charlie," he said, brushing his fingertips across her cheek.

She caught his hand and brought it to her lips, closing her eyes as she kissed his palm. "Yes, you do, Augustus T. Riley."

"Gus," he said.